Spring
of
Spirits

Book Two of the *Seasons of Growing* Series

Kerry E.B. Black

Printed in the United States of America
First Printing 2022

ISBN: 978-1-948894-31-9

Tree Shadow Press

www.treeshadowpress.com

For reproduction permission, contact:

Kerry E. B. Black

https://kerrylizblack.wordpress.com

DEDICATION

Dedicated to all those battling personal demons.

ACKNOWLEDGMENTS

Writing begins as a solitary pursuit, but the hope is it will not end that way. Therefore, I wish to thank my dear and talented friend, Deb, without whom this book wouldn't be published as it is, and Kyle Terry, who all but demanded a second installment in the seasons Casey and her friends experience. And of course, my darling mother, who, as was asserted before, is nothing like Casey's.

CHAPTER ONE:
A SURPRISE HOMECOMING

Since she participated in the autumn equinox ceremony, Casey Adams could tell if someone was about to die, and she mourned for them. Somehow her tears eased their passage to their next existence.

Dreams of the witch came less frequently, but Casey continued to deal with the visions. Life and death persisted without her permission, and she played her unlooked-for part, but this morning, her role as sister and family helper took precedence.

As the sun rose, she stretched away the night's grip and readied for the day. She called to her siblings, "Rise and shine, Sweet Peas."

"Already up, Sleepy Head." Her brother Malcolm zoomed through the hallway clad in a superhero cape and mask.

"Hey, slow down, Crazy Man." Casey scooped him into a hug as he rushed by. "You can't go to school wearing a cape and mask. Teacher would not approve."

He wiggled free and placed hands on his squared hips. "Yeah, but what if a bad guy shows up at school? They'll be glad a superhero is there if a bad guy shows up. I can stop him if I have my cape and mask, but if I don't, what then?"

Casey ruffled his hair. "We'll have to take our chances, I

guess. Besides, you're pretty tough in your civie clothes, you know."

He puffed out his thin chest. "Darned right."

Casey wiped her upper lip to disguise a smile. "Breakfast in five. Okay?"

"What're we having today? Cereal?" Rachel yawned in her doorway.

"Only the finest grains for you." Casey kissed her sister's cheek. "And milk. Mustn't forget the milk."

They laughed and set to the morning's preparations. Hairbrushes and lip gloss littered the sink. The toothpaste leaked from its uncapped tube. Casey sighed and tidied as she went through the daily routine. Pick up and rehang a towel. Straighten the tub mat. Close the shower curtain.

At least she could make noise, though, with Mom away.

When Mom was home, the Adams family scampered about like mice all day long, afraid to wake the dragon's wrath.

As she carried their nightclothes to the laundry basket, Casey froze. Raised voices downstairs. *Dad and a woman.* Casey strained. *Not Mom. Thank goodness. Aunt Hettie! But why did she sound upset?*

With a leaden weight in her stomach, Casey descended to peek into the kitchen. Dad sat in his seat, dejected head in his aging hands.

Aunt Hettie paced. "Where would she have gone?"

Dad shook his head. Gray dulled his locks. "I don't know. Let me think. Okay? I bet she'll be home here in a couple."

Home? Did Mom leave the treatment center?

Aunt Hettie threw her hands into the air. "What's the point of intense therapy if she walks away from it? How'd she get out?"

"I don't know, Hettie. It's not like she was a prisoner. She probably put on her coat and walked out the door.

How're they supposed to know if she's a patient or a visitor?"

Sure don't want to be here for Mom's homecoming.

Heart pounding, Casey rushed back upstairs to hurry her siblings. "We'll get breakfast on the way. I'm driving you to school today."

Rachel dropped a face cloth over a blush brush on the sink top, a sheepish smile dimpling her cheeks. Her voice bubbled, high and guilty. "Won't that make you late for school? What's going on?"

Malcolm thrust his chin into a heroic pose. "Yeah, is there trouble about?"

Casey grabbed their backpacks and coats. "Just want to spend time with you. Now hurry." She tossed their shoes to them.

Malcolm struggled with his laces. Casey stooped and tied them for him.

Malcolm pouted. "Hey, I can do it."

The screen door slammed downstairs.

Hopefully, that's Aunt Hettie on her way to her shift at the diner and not Mom popping by.

Casey tried to ignore her thundering worries. She smiled at her brother. "I know you can, but now it's done. Two perfect, double-knotted bows. See? Now let's get going." She shoved her arms through her coat sleeves, careful of the ripped lining, grabbed her purse, and sprinted down the stairs. "I'll beat you both to the car!"

Malcolm scrambled to catch her. Rachel brought up the rear, disinterested in the outcome of the race.

Only Dad sat at the kitchen table. "Bye, Dad!" Casey kissed his cheeks as she passed. "I'm driving the kids today.

Malcolm mimicked Casey's exit while Rachel swept through in a more stately fashion.

Casey flung open the door to leave. She and her siblings gasped. Their Mom's bulk blocked their exit. A wintry wind swirled her hair about her face like Medusa's snakes. The wind and the myth froze them in place until Mom narrowed her eyes and a dangerous line formed between her brows.

"And where do you think you're going?"

CHAPTER TWO:
OFF TO SCHOOL

Malcolm shuffled behind Casey's legs. Casey stepped aside, using her body to shield Malcolm and Rachel.

"Mom!" She cleared her throat. "What a surprise." Her gaze darted in frantic search for an escape. "We're heading to school of course. We'll see you soon." She motioned with her hand to allow her mother admittance to the kitchen.

Mom made no move.

"Look who's here!" Casey shot a panicked look at her Dad. Her voice pitched high, too bright, near hysterics. "It's Mom! I bet you have lots to talk about."

Mom jammed her fists upon her ample hips.

Casey fumbled with her keys. "Sorry we have to dash. We've got to be going or we'll be super late."

Mom's pinched lips quivered. "You're not going anywhere." She pointed to the kitchen table. "Go sit."

"But Mom..." Casey hated the quaver in her voice.

"Don't 'but Mom' me! Sit." She herded them to the kitchen table with her formidable presence. The kitchen door slammed on their escape.

Casey slid into her seat. Mom assumed her head-of-table position. Dad and Casey exchanged wide-eyed glances. Rachel crossed her arms before her, a moue of displeasure contorting her elvish features. Malcolm wrung his hands and rocked from foot to foot until Casey reached out a comforting hand. He clung to her as though he survived a shipwreck and gripped a life preserver. Casey gave his little fingers a squeeze. He squeezed in response.

"You." Mom pointed at Casey. "You're why I was in therapy." Her breaths came in gasps.

Casey shuddered. *Don't want the kids involved in this mess.* "Malcolm, Rachel, maybe you should get some gloves and scarves and run to the bus stop."

Mom slammed her hands on the table. Its metal supports groaned. Her chair fell back with a crash as she lurched to her feet and yelled, "You're not in charge!" Mom's nostrils flared.

Casey cringed.

Dad used a soft, calming voice as he stood, palms outstretched in supplication. "Honey, we're glad to see you, but please don't yell at Casey. She's a big help around here."

Mom's face darkened. "A big help, huh? Because of her, I've been pushed out of my own home while she lords it up like she's the queen of the castle." She leaned across the table and pointed at Casey. "Do you know what I learned in therapy? There are toxic people. And guess what? Toxic people try to push other people around. Make them do things they don't want or need to do. Things like go to therapy while they take over as head of the home life." Spittle sprayed with each enraged phrase. "Sound like anyone you might know, Casey?"

Yeah. You.

Instead of worsening the situation, Casey stared at her ragged fingernails and said nothing. She composed her face into the bland mask she reserved for such occasions.

Mom's intention to harm herself lingered about her psyche like a spectral shroud. Casey examined it closer with furtive use of what she dubbed her "banshee sense." Patches of it fell away as Mom grew mentally stronger. It may never disappear entirely, but its diminishing status gave Casey hope.

"Mom," Casey studied the metallic specks in the white tabletop. "We're proud of you." Tears blurred the scene. "You're doing the therapy to grow stronger, and I think it's working." She swallowed around the growing lump in her throat. "I know it's hard." Her voice dropped to just above a whisper. "Please don't give up."

Mom leaned over the table until her bosom threatened to burst from the top of her blouse. "You don't know anything. I know what you are. You're a broken little girl who thinks if she pushes attention on other people, nobody will recognize her faults." Mom's breath coated Casey like a noxious cloud. "Well, I see them." She straightened and glared. "Look in a mirror and fix yourself before pointing your accusations at me."

Dad had edged closer to Mom and engulfed her in a squeeze. "Honey, nobody is trying to replace you, especially not Casey." He motioned toward the door. Casey, Rachel, and Malcolm snuck out as he said,

"Didn't you hear what she said? We love you."

Mom's voice cut through the air. "Don't you understand? Casey's a freak. Always has been."

Cold March air slapped her burning face as Casey ushered her little brother into the car. Rachel took the front passenger's seat, and they all closed their doors with care. Casey bit her lip when she turned over the engine, casting fearful glances at the door. She pulled the car into gear and left their house in the rearview mirror.

They drove in silence until Rachel cleared her throat. "How long do you think she'll stay?"

Casey squeezed the steering wheel, unable to answer. Instead she turned on the radio. Some pop singer chirped about a bad break up, and before long, the younger kids sang along. They visited a drive-thru for egg sandwiches and by the time they reached the elementary school, color had returned to their faces. Casey wished them a blessed day and waved as they skipped into the stream of grade schoolers on the way inside.

Casey turned off the radio and thumped her head against the steering wheel. *I know I shouldn't, but right now, I hate her. But wait. Why shouldn't I? My own mother hates me. Blames me for her sickness. Maybe I should hate her.*

Casey's stomach gave a painful lurch. *That's it, isn't it? I'm not allowed to hate her because she's sick. None of it's her fault. There's some imbalance, and I'm supposed to just forgive her every meanness.*

Hot tears cooled before they reached her chin. Her phone alarm warned she needed to be on her way to class, so she brushed them away.

As she reached for the radio knob, Casey's heart lurched.

Not now. Please.

The crossing guard outside the entry gates had waved to Casey on her way to her car. From her smiling mouth spurted blood in dark clots. Her hand dropped from her wrist to disappear into a drift of snow. Blood splashed an accompaniment, staining the snow like a twisted Italian Ice. A deep purple mask, discolored eyes swelling shut in the crossing guard's kind, disfigured face.

Car crash?

A sob ripped through Casey. She forced a smile but suspected it resembled a grimace of pain because she ached. A moan joined her sobs.

"Please be with that dear soul," she prayed to she wasn't sure who. "Guide her along her passage." Casey curled into a ball of misery, knees drawn to her chest, hair obscuring the agonized contortions of her grief. "Let my tears ease her as she journeys to her next life."

Casey hugged her knees and rocked. Her choked prayers and pitiful cries muffled the squeal of brakes rendered useless on an icy patch. She jolted at the metallic crunch of impact.

As she felt the soul of the smiling crossing guard pass on, Casey dialed 911.

"There's a car crash." She struggled to keep her voice steady as she gave the address and joined the crowd of would-be helpers in their futile attempt to provide comfort until paramedics arrived.

Something prickled along her spine, a premonition not of death but of danger. A man in the crowd stared at her with angry interest and a strange intensity. Something in his movements brought Rom to mind, Rom her one-time classmate, the misguided lunatic who interpreted his calling with a murderous rampage. Rom, whose hands she could feel around her neck every time she rested upon her pillow.

CHAPTER THREE:
MEETING FRIENDS

By the time Casey left the scene of the accident and arrived at the Ol' Nor'Eastern University campus, she'd missed her first class. She used the visor mirror to re-apply a layer of camouflage. She might see death and ease those about to journey its cold path, but she didn't need to look like death's incarnation. At least not when she was about to meet up with her boyfriend, Tim, and her best friend, Jaimie.

After a final swipe of eyeliner, she grabbed her book bag and headed to the on-campus coffee shop, The Brew Two, and her waiting friends.

Tim's hug felt like home should, safe and welcoming, and Casey nestled her frigid nose to better take in his scent.

"You're freezing, beautiful. Let me get your coffee." Tim hurried to the barista and ordered a triple shot caramel mocha with extra froth, the way Casey took her coffee here.

Jaimie's embrace felt like a massage chair at a mall. Jaimie perpetually moved, ever since she, Casey, and five of their friends, Tim included, had participated in an awakening ceremony last autumn. Jaimie had explained her agitation as a necessity. "I feel out of my element, like a fish on land," she explained. But when she moved, she gathered enough air.

"It's hard to believe spring's coming, isn't it?" Jaimie glared at a snow squall outside the shop's window. "Stupid frozen north."

Tim returned with a fragrant, steaming mug of coffee which Casey wrapped her cold fingers around, grateful.

"Thanks, Tim." She rested her head against his solid chest and sighed. They slid into seats near Jaimie, sipped their drinks, and held hands.

"What's going on with you, girlie?" Jaimie's foot jiggled.

Casey unzipped her coat. "Not much. Why?"

Tim ran a finger along the back of her hand. "You're not worried about," he lowered his voice to a rumbling whisper, "the spring equinox, are you?"

Guess that's coming up soon, huh? "Not really. Are you?"

Tim and Jaimie both shrugged. "Nah," Tim said. "Not really. I mean, we're not going to any god-forsaken ceremonies or anything, so I think we're okay."

No trips to the hills overlooking campus for a ceremony. No bonfire sending secrets to the stars. No disturbing new aspects of themselves awakened by an ancient wisdom, be it a witch or a goddess. Casey shuddered.

"You sure you're okay, Case? You look like you've

seen a ghost." Jaimie rested her elbows on the table. "Shit, you didn't, did you? I mean, see another vision?"

Casey buried her face in Tim's shoulder.

"Oh, honey." Tim embraced her.

Jaimie stroked her hair. "I could tell something was up. I've not seen you this agitated in a while." She patted the table and drew Casey's attention. "You can't do that to yourself, though."

Casey furrowed her brow but avoided eye contact. "It's not like I have any control of it."

Jaimie touched Casey's hand and whispered, "Not the vision. I know you can't help that. But Casey, you shouldn't harm yourself."

"Harm myself?" *What's she talking about?*

Jaimie squeezed her hand. "You've been doing so well. I hate seeing the scratches again."

Scratches? She'd been raking her nails across her arms and chest without realizing it. *Shoot.* She pulled up her sleeve. Her nails had left red tracks from elbow to wrist. *Jaimie's right. I haven't done this in a long time. Not since ...* Her heart thumped heavy realization *... Mom went away.*

Tim pulled her into a tighter embrace. "What's going on?"

Casey studied the snaking grain of the tabletop rather than look into their eyes. She licked her lips and willed the words. They came out as a hoarse whisper. "My mother came home this morning. Checked herself out, I'm guessing."

Jaimie covered her gaping mouth, eyes wide.

Tim lifted Casey's chin with a gentle finger. "And I'm guessing that's not a good thing."

Jaimie snorted and looked away.

Tim bit his lip. He sounded hurt. "You don't talk about her much, so I don't know."

Tears blurred Casey's view. "She hates me."

Tim's face contorted with alarm. "No. Nobody could hate you, Casey."

He believes that. In his estimation, nobody would humiliate a troubled girl. Nobody, especially not her own mother, would wish her harm. Tim's love-filled world could not admit such hate.

He couldn't be more wrong.

Casey lingered over her coffee, inhaling its spicy warmth. "Jaimie, did your roommate ever return?"

Jaimie drummed her fingers along her coffee cup. "Nope. She dropped out after autumn semester. Why?"

Words stuck in Casey's throat. *What if she hates the idea?* "Do you want a roommate?"

Jaimie shrugged. "I guess so. I mean, they're going to assign one to me pretty soon." She sighed and drooped her head over the chair back, the picture of suffering. "I just hope she won't be weird."

Casey cleared her throat. "What would you look for in a roommate?"

"You know, non-smoker, respectful of personal space and property, friendly, cool. Why?"

Heat rose in Casey's face. *Don't stop now.* "I don't know. I mean, how expensive is it to board here?" She traced the table's wood grain with her finger. "Do they fold it in to your student loans?"

"It's part of it." Jaimie paused her tapping and gaped. "Wait, are you thinking of rooming?"

Casey shrugged. "If I could afford it, and if it would be okay at home." *If the kids would be okay. Mom might improve if she's not always angry at me.*

"Oh my gosh, Case," Jaimie grabbed her hand again, "that would be the best thing ever! I'd love to have you as a roommate!"

Casey blinked back tears.

Jaimie smiled, bouncing with enthusiasm. "You'd need to talk to the Bursar and Student Housing. They're in the same building. I'll walk you there now if you want."

Casey chuckled and brushed away a tear escapee. "You have class to attend now. I can walk to the admissions building myself."

Tim opened his mouth to protest.

Casey set a finger on his lips. "You, too. You have your 'Intro to Criminal Justice' class, and you can't miss it." She flexed her inconsequential muscles, blushed, and giggled. "I may be small, but I am mighty. After all, I can take down a serial killer with one well-placed knee."

Tim's eyes sparkled, and a smile played on his lips. "You are tough, all right, and serial killers should steer clear."

Jaimie looked at the time on her cell phone. "Well, I guess we'd better get going or we will be late for class. Dr. Petrine is discussing the impact of Rachel Carson's research on our agriculture, and I don't want to miss it. Carson's one of my heroes." She hugged Casey. "Let me know when you're moving in, okay?"

"I'm looking into it, Jaimie. I don't know for sure yet."

Jaimie grabbed her backpack and waved. "I know. Just hoping you'll move in soon." Her hair swished behind her as she exited and hurried along the cobblestone path.

Tim removed and tied his scarf in a loose knot around Casey's neck. His cologne engulfed her. "You stay safe, my beautiful girl."

Casey stood on tiptoes to kiss him. The touch sent an electric jolt through her, and she sighed.

He brushed a lock of her hair behind her ear. "I love you. Let me know if you need to talk."

Casey nodded. "I will. Promise." She grabbed her bookbag. "Now get going. Education awaits."

His gaze lingered, but she shooed him. "I'll see you at lunch."

They took separate paths to their destinations.

CHAPTER FOUR:
ROOMMATE

The gum-chewing receptionist eyed Casey, twirling her blue-tipped hair. "Do you have an appointment?"

Casey shook her head and tapped slush from her boot. "No. Sorry." She screwed up her courage to engage in further conversation when all she'd rather do was curl into a ball in some safe place and see no one. "But I have a friend looking for a roommate. Her name's Jaimie, and we'd like to share a dorm room."

Blue-tips blew and popped a bubble. "Doesn't matter. Someone's already back there." She peeked to see if they were alone. She whispered, "Housing troubles." She shook her head, chin in the lead, as though Casey should understand her meaning.

She didn't.

A gust of cold air accompanied a young woman's entrance.

Casey's breath froze within her.

The woman might have been twenty years old, pretty despite premature worry lines and a few strands of silver in her dark hair. Bags hung heavy beneath her eyes, and she frowned. "I'm here for the meeting."

"Deirdre Lowry?" Blue-tips jabbed her black-painted thumbnail toward the door. "Yeah, they're waiting for you."

Casey rubbed her eyes in the hopes of clearing her vision. *Please, no.* The scene remained unaltered. The young woman, a fellow student, wore the veil of suicidal intentions. Casey allowed her senses to expand. The girl had considered slitting her wrists and ankles, but she'd collected a stockpile of pills. She kept them in a tote beneath her loft bed.

Tears roiled within Casey, a tempest ready to erupt. Casey pushed emotions down and composed herself, though her heart pounded and her knees wobbled.

Just don't throw up. Every time you get upset, you vomit.

Fear for the young woman overruled social awkwardness. She pointed to the door and asked Blue-tips, "What are they meeting for?"

Blue-tips rested her chewing chin on her crossed arms. "I'm not supposed to say, so don't repeat anything. See, the girl already in there, Amber, filed a bunch of complaints, said she can't endure another minute as that new girl's roommate. Amber's parents are in there, too, and they looked pissed. Said they'd sue the school because their darling was having so much distress and her grades are suffering. Here's the thing, though. I'm in that Amber girls' classes. She's nice enough, but she's not the best student, if you know what I mean. So, I'm thinking this new girl's some sort of scapegoat." She slow-nodded again, "I feel kind of bad for the new girl. Deirdre, I mean. See, where's she supposed to go? The dorms are full."

This disappointment and rejection might make her take those pills.

Muffled yells from the office indicated things heated up within. A deep, male voice yelled, "My attorney." The door burst open. A man and woman thundered through the office, pursued by a girl about Casey's age. "Guys, wait. Please." She turned back to the room and yelled, "Why don't you just cooperate? Stay with a friend or something, Deirdre Lowry. You obviously don't like me any more than I like you."

A tired-sounding man emerged and blocked the entry with his body. "That's enough, Amber."

Tears erupted from Amber, and she ran after her parents.

The man rubbed his eyes before looking up at the Blue-tipped receptionist with a sigh. "Has any room turned up empty? Please tell me we've overlooked something."

Blue-tips popped another bubble. "Huh-uh, Mr. Kean. Just that room in Women's South where the freshman went awol."

Casey steeled herself. *My cue.* She cleared her throat. "Excuse me, that's why I came, actually. I believe you're talking about my friend Jaimie's room. She and I would like to room together, but I need to find out..."

"Sorry." The man, Mr. Kean, straightened and regarded Casey from his greater height. "That room's been assigned." He nodded toward the exit and tapped on the receptionist's desk. "See to the paperwork for Ms. Amber Jacobson immediately, please."

Blue-tips huffed, but nodded. "Yes, sir."

He took a step toward his office door but stopped

before touching the handle. He tapped his foot. "I think I'll take a coffee break." He motioned toward the office with his head and lowered his voice. "Break the news to Ms. Lowry, will you Constance?"

Constance Blue-tips' mouth dropped open. Her gum fell to the desktop. "Seriously?"

He left without a backward look.

Constance threw her gum into the waste bin. It made a little thump, and she muttered, "Coward."

Casey edged toward the exit. *No reason to be here any longer, I guess.*

"Hey." Constance pushed back from the desk and approached Casey. She touched Casey's arm, ignoring Casey's little jump at the contact. With a conspiratorial glance at the office door, she whispered, "You wanted a room on campus, right? I think I have an idea."

Casey wiggled from Constance's grip. She rubbed the spot as though to wipe away Constance's touch. "Oh?"

"Yeah. See, there's nothing wrong with Deirdre Lowry in there. She's just a bit - odd. Different. You know?" Constance's gaze bore into Casey until Casey ducked her chin, unable to maintain eye contact. Constance crossed her arms over her chest. "Yeah, I think you get what I'm saying." She clicked her tongue. "The way I see it, little Ms. Amber is a bit entitled and completely coddled by her Mummy and Daddy. Instead of working through their differences, she insisted on a room change. Well, she'll win. She'll room with your friend. In the meantime," Constance jabbed a thumb over her shoulder to the office, "Poor Lowry gets to think there's something wrong with her.

That she's the problem," Constance huffed. "She's not. At least I don't believe it."

Casey stole a glance at the office. Within, a girl with suicidal intentions waited to discover her fate. Casey's throat tightened.

"So what do you say?" Constance reached for Casey but stopped short of touching when Casey recoiled. "I think it would be good for you all. Besides, Lowry's room's in the updated hall, while your friend's room's in the old wing." She raised her eyebrows and smiled.

Casey studied Constance's feet. Mismatched socks just peeked above the tops of her worn tennies. *Not good shoes for this kind of weather. Wonder if she changes to boots?*

"Hello?" Constance tapped her foot.

Casey tried to raise her gaze and made it as far as Constance's collar. "I don't know if I can." Heat rose in her cheeks. "I needed to ask if I can afford it."

Constance pulled out a chair. "Have a seat, please. Let's fill out some paperwork. I happen to know of a really great unclaimed scholarship that might be exactly what we need to make this happen."

Casey's head spun. *This is happening so fast.* "What do you mean?"

"Let's just say I'm a good Samaritan, okay?" She tapped the papers. "Now fill this out while I talk to our friend in the other room."

She strode into the office. "So, that was a bit more excitement than necessary this early in the morning, don't you think?" Her brash tone took on a softness. "No, please don't cry. Listen, it's not worth it. Really. If she's that much of a prat, you're better off without her as a roommate." Constance sat beside Deirdre Lowry and slid an arm around her shaking shoulders. "Please don't cry." She handed her a box of tissues. "We're working on a new roommate for you, and I bet you'll like this one."

Deirdre scowled over her reddened nose. "Is it that girl out there?" She pointed at Casey.

Constance patted Dierdre's shoulder. "Yep. She's really nice. You'll like her. Promise. See, she's filling out the paperwork as we speak."

Casey picked a pen from a "Buffy the Vampire Slayer" mug and read the page. The words on the paper blurred as she processed all that happened that day.

What did I just get myself into?

CHAPTER FIVE:
STRANGE ROLES

"What do you mean?" Jaimie's face paled and flushed by turns.

Casey gulped. "It happened so fast. They said they had someone assigned to you."

"I thought we were going to be roommates. I didn't want a stranger. I wanted you. That was the plan."

Casey shivered. "Please don't be angry at me. I couldn't do anything else."

"Damn it, Casey, who's it going to be? This new roommate? Is it some sorority wannabe? A type-A personality who's going to freak out if I leave a bra out of place? A slob, maybe, who'll make me look like a neat-nic? Seriously, I'm freaking out here!"

"Amber somebody-or-other. Jacobson, I think."

Jaimie pushed back in her chair. "Amber Jacobson?" She scrunched up her forehead. "She was in my anthropology class during summer semester." She tapped the tabletop with her fingernails.

The familiar rhythm comforted Casey. Jaimie's taps and bounces were her signature.

Jaimie punctuated their ditty with a slap from her palms. "She was alright."

Casey heaved a sigh, relieved. "I'm so glad."

Jaimie grabbed Casey's hand. "But does that mean you won't be staying here? Oh, Casey, I hoped you could get away from your home for a bit."

Casey's eyes darted faster than her guilty feelings. She whispered, "I may move in this weekend, if the scholarship goes through."

Jaimie gaped. "What? That's great! Where'll you be staying? Women's hall, of course, but where?"

"West. The room Amber's leaving."

Before they could say anything more, Tim stomped snow from his boots, kissed the top of Casey's head, and joined them. "Some say Spring is in the air. I say those people are sadly mistaken."

"Tim, Casey's moving in, but not as my roomie. She dumped me for somebody new."

Casey chewed her lip. *Is she joking, or is she upset? She's smiling, but her words sound hurt.*

Tim raised his eyebrows. "Oh yeah?"

Jaimie grasped Casey's hand. "It's okay, though, Casey'll be on campus, so we'll be able to see more of her."

A wave of relief rushed through Casey. *She's not mad. Thank Heavens.* "I won't know for a while if my scholarship application was accepted. Without it, I can't stay here."

Jaimie flapped her hands dismissively. "Yes, well, I have a feeling you'll be here this semester." Her smile spread wide. "And we'll be able to do all sorts of things together. It will be so fun!"

Casey looked down at her hands and sniffed. "I

really wanted to be your roommate, Jaimie."

Jaimie patted Casey's hand. "I know you did. I love you, Case." She squeezed Casey's hand before she let go and eased back into her seat. "Even if you did abandon me for someone new."

Casey opened her mouth to protest.

Tim hugged her. "Jaimie's teasing you!"

Her friends laughed. Casey chuckled to be a part of their mirth, but she didn't understand. Not entirely. *Friendships have such strange rules, and I don't always know them.*

After hasty farewells, they rushed to their classes. Lectures, assignments, and a quiz drained Casey. She dragged herself to her car and, sighing, sunk into its upholstery. She pressed play on her Tchaikovsky CD and allowed the swell of the orchestra to ease her anxiety.

CHAPTER SIX:
DOWN A CEMETERY PATH

When she pulled up to her house, she opted not to park in the driveway. *Dad's car isn't here.* Casey scratched beneath her coat sleeve. *Suppose Mom's still there and angrier than this morning.* The dashboard clock drew her attention. *The kids should be getting off the activity bus soon. If I take my time, I can meet them at the bus stop and walk them home. Wonder if they heard about the crossing guard?*

She tied Tim's scarf tight about her throat and began her journey. His cedar cologne scented the fabric and wrapped her in a feeling of safety and wellbeing. She meandered along Sage Drive until she reached Rosemary, a longer trip than heading straight up Basil to the bus stop, but she had time to kill. Rosemary boasted fewer houses and an old cemetery.

At the cemetery gate, patches of yellow and violet broke through murky snow drifts. Casey bent and touched the delicate crocus petals. She took photos with her cellular and sent copies to Tim and Jaimie with the hashtag "signs of spring. Don't give up hope."

A whine drew her attention. Just inside the cemetery gates, a bedraggled black dog hunkered. Its massive head rested on dessert-plate sized paws. Heavy eyebrows hung over entreating brown eyes.

The dog's whimper tore at Casey's heart. She hunched to make a cautious approach. She kept her voice low and level. "Good boy. What are you doing here in the cold? Are you hurt?"

The dog sniffed her hand with the caution of a stray, never close enough to touch, before it turned and padded along the cemetery walkway. It stopped a few paces in and turned with an entreaty and whimper.

"Do you want me to follow?"

The dog capered and wagged its tail.

Casey glanced at her phone. *Still time to meet the kids.* "I'm coming."

Old snow crunched beneath her hiking boots, but the dog progressed soundlessly through the monuments and tombstones. The path split. Newer, flat stones marked graves to the left. The dog took the path to the right where imposing marble structures dating from the late 1700's and 1800's reigned. When Casey paused, the dog looked over its massive haunch and whimpered.

"Coming." *Wonder if I'll find Timmy in a well, like in that old black-and-white show "Lassie" that Aunt Mae used to like so much.* She shivered. *Strange to think of bubbly Aunt Mae still and in the ground.* Her gaze swept the graves.

The dog lay on the ground beneath a massive birch tree. Its nose twitched toward a hole in the stone wall of a small crypt.

A plaintive cry quieter than the whispered breezes emanated from within.

Casey felt the pull, an irresistible requirement to mourn a living being as it passed to its next plane of existence. She'd been told her tears cleared the path for the departing soul. *Is there a person trapped in there?* Tears flowed hot from Casey to cool on her cheeks. She knelt by the crypt, ignoring the cold as it melted into her weathered jeans. She leaned onto her hands for a better view.

It's too dark. She lit her cell phone. Something within reflected its light. *An animal? Yes.*

She looked over her shoulder at the dog. It thumped its furry tail against the ground. Her voice shook with suppressed emotion. "Do you want me to cry for your friend?"

Thump, thump, thump went its tail.

Casey squinted into the darkness. Grey fur with silver and black stripes. A cat. Casey shimmied her hand into the hole. *The poor thing might attack me.* But it didn't. It accepted her touch and purred with a broken rhythm. Snot blackened nostrils desperate for oxygen flared. Casey hummed her agony until the cat took a last, shuddering breath. *Rest in peace, little one.*

She wiped her eyes. The intense melancholy lifted when the animal passed. She sniffed. "Am I a psychopomp for animals, too, then?" She reached to embrace the black dog, but it skittered outside her range.

"It's okay." She raised her hands in surrender. "I don't like being touched either. At least, not until I know the person really well." She wiped an errant tear and tilted her head at the dog. "Do you want to come with me? I'm meeting my kid sister and brother. They'd love to meet you. We've all wanted a pet. Mom says we can't have one, though."

The dog stood and shook. Black fur floated from him only to resettle into its coat. It pattered away, its big feet did not disturb the snow with its passage and left no prints.

Casey wiped her nose. "Fine, then. I'll just be on my way."

At the bus stop, she watched birds chatter in nearby tree branches laden with tight buds like chartreuse confetti. She snapped another photo and labeled it as before, but she added, "See, I told you. Spring will be here before we know it."

Spring. Another Equinox. Something inside her panged with worry. It was a ceremony during the last autumn equinox that caused all the trouble before. Because of it, she now could tell when someone was about to die. She had no choice but mourn their passing.

The bus pulled to a squealed stop and whoosh of emissions. Malcolm burst from the door as soon as it opened and flung himself at Casey. "Sister! It's you!"

"Brother!" She kissed his cheek.

He pulled away and wiped his cheek. "Yuck, Casey." He side-mouthed, "The guys are watching."

She laughed and resisted the urge to ruffle his hair. "Sorry."

Rachel leaned against a stop sign and shook her head.

"Hey, where's your hat, Malcolm?"

He grunted and pointed to his backpack as he bent to lift it.

"That backpack doesn't have ears that need warming, so the hat's not doing it any good stuffed inside." Rachel adjusted her own knitted cap until the puffball atop fell like a ponytail.

"Hand 'em over. You've carried these burdens long enough for today." Casey gathered their backpacks, noting the wear. *They need new ones. These will be splitting before the end of the school year.* She wiggled her eyebrows at them. "At least until we get home and you do your homework." Casey led them down Rosemary. *No point hurrying home. Don't know how Mom's going to be.*

They jabbered about school days and gym class and teachers they all knew. Nobody mentioned the crossing guard or her fatal accident. The crisp air reddened their cheeks and noses as they approached the cemetery gates. The big dog stood in the entry and eyed their passage.

Casey nodded to it.

Rachel put her hands on her hips and frowned. She looked from the cemetery to Casey.

Casey giggled at her sister. *She looks like an angry elf with mismatched gloves.* "What?"

Rachel shook her head and thundered ahead of them, head tucked to avoid the wind.

Malcolm widened his eyes. "What's wrong with her?"

They trudged behind Rachel.

Casey shrugged. "Don't know. Maybe she doesn't like dogs."

"Dogs? What's dogs got to do with anything?"

Casey glanced over her shoulder. The dog sat still as a sentry just inside the cemetery gate. Casey spun

Malcolm. "Him."

Malcolm tilted his head and stood on tippy toes. "Him who?"

The dog blinked slow and wise.

Oh no. They can't see him. Casey shuddered. *Great.* She cleared her throat. "I saw a dog."

CHAPTER SEVEN:
TOO WARM A WELCOME

Casey moved the car into the driveway and lingered over cleaning it out. She hid the keys in the inner pocket of her backpack. *In case Mom decides she wants to go for a spin. Can't find keys. Can't drive.*

The screen door slam announced their arrival. *Should have traded out the screen for the storm door, but hey, spring's almost here now, so little point in that.* Heat accosted them. Rachel removed her coat and gloves with stealthy movements, as though afraid rapid movements or loud noises might provoke an attack.

Malcolm, however, yelled, "Wow wee! Why's it so hot in here?" He peeled off winter wear and left a trail of knit as he climbed a chair to check the thermostat. "Is this thing broken? It says it's nine zero F. Should it be?"

Casey repeated, "90 degrees? No, I'll fix it. The thermostat must have been bumped."

Before she touched the dial, an all-too-human growl of disapproval made her stomach drop. "Don't.

Touch. That."

Casey froze. Malcolm grabbed her collar, eyes saucers in his pale face.

Mother.

"Don't you like the welcoming warmth, Casey Prissy?"

Dressed in a sequined top and gray stretch jogging pants, her graying hair escaping a pile atop her head, Mom leaned into the kitchen. Her deodorant had failed, and sweat smeared her makeup.

"Oh, I didn't realize you set it this way. Sorry, Mom." Careful to avoid locking gazes with her, Casey shooed the kids. "Let's get upstairs and get our homework done." She glanced over her shoulder at the stain on Mom's belly. Grape jelly, most likely, fowled the silver shine. "We'll keep out of your hair and quiet, okay?"

With a voice like a small rockslide, Mom said, "No. It's. Not. Okay." She stomped over to the back stairwell and blocked their exit. "I've not seen you kids in an eternity."

A month. One glorious month.

"I've been a captive at that looney bin. Mistreated. Ridiculed. Half-starved."

Look plenty well-fed to me.

Rachel stomped. "Stop it, Mom. We came to see you on Sunday."

"Not all of you." Mom frowned at Casey.

Casey mumbled, "I worked at the library on Sunday. We had a new shipment to catalogue." Casey's cheeks burned. *Besides, I didn't think you'd miss me.*

"And where was Hettie? She'll go driving off to other

states to help other people, but when her own sister's in the hospital..."

Casey felt a surge of anger, and her voice shook. *How dare she! Aunt Hettie's been here almost every day since Mom went to that treatment center, just trying to help though she could barely keep on her feet from exhaustion.* "Aunt Hettie was working a double shift. You know she always picks up extra hours on Sundays. That's when tour buses pass through on their way back to wherever they started. Good tips, usually."

Mom's eyes welled up, and her paunchy cheeks trembled. "You see how she speaks to me? What I have to put up with?" She pointed a quavering finger at Casey. "How sharper than a serpent's tooth it is to have a thankless child!"

Rachel, puffed up though she was, only reached Mom's belly. "*King Lear*, huh? Well, Shakespeare also said, 'The oldest bore most.'"

Casey gasped. *She's reading King Lear? She's only ten.*

Rachel's cheeks blazed brilliant red. "Why are you so mean to Casey, Momma? What did she ever do to deserve you hating her?"

Mom sputtered, "Me? Mean?"

Malcolm slid behind Casey. His hand in hers felt icy despite the heat.

Mom's going to kill Rachel.

"Rachel," Casey's head ached. *Why can't their mother be normal?* "You don't need to defend me." She pleaded into the silence with worry-filled eyes. *Drop it. I don't want you hurt.* "Mom, I hope when you've finished your time with the doctors, you feel differently."

"I'm done with doctors and their crackpot ideas. I'm done with hospitals and medicines that make me feel like a zombie. And I'm done with you, you miserable bitch! You've turned them against me! My sweet little children hate me because of you!" She pointed, her eyes clouded with rage.

"No, they don't hate you." Casey pushed Rachel behind her. Malcolm released Casey's hand, probably to grab Rachel's. "We all love you. We just want you to be well again."

"By the way," Mom's head bobbed, and a smirk crossed her lips. "The school called. Seems your scholarship went through. You can move in tomorrow if you want."

Rachel gasped. "Move?"

"Yes, Rachel. Your replacement Momma is looking for a way to fly the coop. Doesn't care about you as much as you thought, does she?" She chuckled. "Makes you wonder why she wants to push me out so badly, doesn't it?"

Casey sighed. "We don't want to push you out. Can't you see? With treatment..."

Mom leaned close enough for spittle to spray on Casey's face. "Didn't you hear me? That hospital isn't helping."

Rachel burst from behind Casey, pulling Malcolm along. "You're not even half through the treatment plan."

Casey grabbed Rachel's shoulder, "Go upstairs, Rachel. Take Malcolm and don't come back until I tell you. Now."

Rachel's lip trembled. Malcolm hid his face in his

elbow.

Casey never saw the blow, but stars blinded her after it landed. She pitched into the kids. She scrambled to keep them upright. *What hit me? Are Rachel and Malcolm okay?*

Rachel screamed, "Mom!"

Malcolm wailed. "Casey, are you okay?"

When Rachel touched a finger to the back of Casey's head, Casey winced.

Rachel stared at her reddened hand. She breathed the words "What did you do?" with disbelief.

Blood trickled around Casey's ear and into her mouth, metallic and sticky. Mom held a chair aloft, eyes and mouth wide. Traces of Casey's hair dangled like guilt from the metal legs.

With a far-away voice, Casey asked, "Why'd you hit me?"

CHAPTER EIGHT:
PHONE CALLS AND HEADWRAPS

Casey jumped when the chair clatter behind her. Mom shuffled into the living room. The couch springs groaned as she flopped into it.

Rachel handed Casey a tea towel. "Get some ice, Malcolm"

Casey touched her sister's cheek. "Thank you, darling."

Rachel's face paled when Casey wobbled to a stand. "Case..."

"It'll be okay." *As soon as the world stops spinning.* "Let me get this cleaned up and take some medicine so I can think what to do next."

Casey stumbled up the stairs while Rachel and Malcolm trailed behind. She found a bottle of pain reliever in the medicine cabinet, cupped some water from the bathroom sink, and swallowed two pills. "I'll lay down for a couple of minutes until these little buddies start to work." She shook the bottle before replacing it.

The kids followed her into her bedroom.

"Casey, your head's still bweeding." Malcolm stuck his thumb in his mouth, a habit he had given up two years earlier.

Casey put the ice and tea towel on her bed and rested her wound atop. "It'll quit soon." She closed her eyes to keep the room from spinning.

Rachel wrung her hands. "Maybe you should go to the hospital. You might need sewn up or something."

Casey reached into her back pocket and removed her phone. She texted Dad. "Are you almost home?" *Please be almost home.* The scene spun, and Casey's stomach lurched.

"Case?" Rachel's worry played across her face with paleness and furrows. "What about the hospital?"

Casey took Rachel's hand. "I can't drive right now."

Rachel chewed her lip. "I can call 9-1-1."

Casey gave her hand a squeeze. "I can't afford an ambulance trip."

Rachel groaned.

"I'll be okay until Daddy gets home. Who knows? I might be all better before he gets here."

The phone jingled. Rachel grabbed it. "I'll read the message for you. You rest." She sighed. "It's from Jaimie, not Dad. Says she'll meet her new roommate in the morning. She's nervous."

Malcolm handed Casey his teddy bear. "Hug him, Casey. He'll help you not hurt." He whispered, "He helps me."

Casey pulled her brother to her. "Thank you. I love you."

"I love you, Casey." He hugged the bear. "Pwease don't die."

Die? How bad do I look? "Can you please bring me

that mirror? The one on my desk."

Malcolm brought the mirror.

Blood matted her hair and smeared along her left cheek. Tiredness circled her eyes like puffy, dark slugs, but no death masked her features. *Banshee sense says I'll live.* She dabbed at the blood on her face. "I'm not dying, little brother."

Her phone jingled again. Rachel pursed her lips. "It's not Daddy. Why doesn't he answer?" She squinted at the screen as though willing her father's response, her thumbs tapping.

"Casey," Rachel cleared her throat. "Are you really leaving us?"

Chills raced up Casey's spine despite the ridiculous heat billowing from the floor vents. "Sweetheart, I was looking into staying on campus, but I'd never leave you." She ignored the dizziness and pushed to a seated position.

"We'd be by ourselves. You know, after school and everything. Unless," she shivered, "Momma was home."

I've been so selfish. "I won't leave you alone with her. Please don't worry."

Casey's phone rang. Rachel answered. "Hi, Tim. This is Casey's sister, Rachel. I'm okay. Well, sorta. That's why I texted, though. Yeah, could you please drive my sister to the doctor's?"

Casey's mouth fell open. "Rachel, I didn't ask you to call Tim." She heard Tim's response of "On my way."

The phone jingled another text notification. "It's Dad. He'll be home in about an hour. Should I tell him what happened?"

Casey shrugged. "No point now, really, if you two

cuties come with me to the hospital. Tim'll be here before Dad's home." *No point upsetting him when he's still at work.* "We'll leave a note."

Malcolm blanched. "What about Momma?"

"I guess I could text Aunt Hettie." Casey struggled to focus on the tiny keyboard.

Rachel sighed. "Give it here. I'll text her." As she typed, Rachel pursed her lips. "You know, I need my own phone." She set the phone on her sister's bedside table. "Especially if you're jumping ship. I mean, what if I need to dial the police or ambulance or something."

Casey nodded. "That's a very good point."

Rachel bent and checked the melting ice pack under Casey. "I'll be back."

The answer from Aunt Hettie wavered slightly as Casey struggled to focus, "I'm on the way. Leave as soon as Tim gets there. Don't wait for me, and let me know you're ok after."

Rachel returned with a fresh tea towel wrapped around a bag of frozen peas. "Hold this on your head."

"Rach, did you bump your mouth?" Casey gently touched her sister's cheek.

Rachel pulled away. "Yeah. I'm all right, though. Should we go outside and wait for Tim?"

"Sure." They crept down the stairs.

As they passed the living room, they heard Mom sobbing into her pillow. Rachel scowled and whispered, "Do you think she'll ever get well again? I mean, for real?"

Casey studied the peeling paint in the hallway before ushering the kids outside.

Not if she doesn't follow the doctors' advice.

No sooner had the screen door pounded shut than

Tim peeled into the driveway. He left the engine running as he jumped to help Casey inside. "My poor girl." After Casey buckled her seat belt, he asked, "Are we taking the kids?" Worry wrinkled his brow. "I don't have a car seat."

Rachel touched his elbow. "Our Aunt Hettie's on her way. You go. Take care of our girl."

CHAPTER NINE:
UNIVERSITY HOSPITAL

Tim parked in the emergency room lot. "Do you need a wheelchair?"

"No." *Seriously?* Despite her bravado, Casey leaned against the car until the dizziness passed.

Tim ran to the curb and brought a wheelchair with a big number 7 painted on its back. "I know you're okay, but if you fall, you could injure yourself more." He rested a big hand on her shoulder. "Please, don't be stubborn. It's a temporary situation."

Casey rolled her eyes at him. "Fine." She sat and allowed him to push her. He rubbed her shoulder as she checked in and presented her insurance card.

When asked how long they should anticipate for a wait, the intake nurse leaned forward like a conspirator and whispered, "You have a bleeding head injury. They'll call you soon." She raised her eyebrows as though they'd won a prize.

They exchanged confused glances, but Tim replied, "Um, thanks."

When they sat, Casey rested her head against Tim's

shoulder. "It's like I'm sucking out all your heat." She closed her eyes to the spinning world and all the injured people in the uncomfortable ER waiting room chairs.

Tim kissed her temple. "You can have all my warmth if it helps." He wrapped an arm around her shoulder, and she nestled closer. A team of cheerful reporters droned local news on the television. Their banter faded, and Casey dozed.

In her dream, the witch stood at the sliding door of the ER, beckoning with long-nailed fingers, her flowing white gown buffeted by an unworldly breeze. This witch had haunted Casey's dreams since she participated in the autumn equinox ceremony months ago, as she'd frequented the dreams of all the participants. Foreboding gripped Casey's insides, and as ever when in the dark-haired banshee's presence, Casey worried she'd vomit.

"Casey!" The witch woman's smile revealed too many teeth surrounded by crimson lips. Red rimmed her eyes as though she spent most of her life in tears, but she glowed with inner beauty. "You're about to meet a friend."

Tim jostled her awake. "Honey, they're ready for you." He rubbed her shoulder.

She blinked in the glare of artificial lights and tried to remember where she was and how she'd gotten there. Her head throbbed, and Tim held a tea towel stained with blood. *Oh yeah. That's my blood. Mom hit me on the head.*

They followed a woman in purple scrubs through doors so similar to those in Casey's dream that Casey shivered. Wary, she answered questions on a clipboard. No, she did not blackout. Yes, she was experiencing headache, nausea, and fatigue. Some dizziness. Although she had some fogginess, she did not have amnesia.

When Casey bent her head for a quick examination of the wound, the nurse whistled. "Oh, honey, how'd you get this gash?"

Casey stiffened. "How?" *What do I say? My wacko mother slammed me with a kitchen chair?* "Um," she hesitated then with eyes wide as Aunt Mae's pecan pies, Casey silently pleaded for a solution from Tim.

Tim's mouth popped open, but he remained silent.

The nurse cleared her throat. "Well, you're going to have to step outside, please." She opened the curtain and raised an eyebrow at Tim. "Ms. Adams needs to don a hospital gown."

Tim wavered. "Uh, where should I go?"

"Do you remember how to get to the waiting room? It's down this hallway," she motioned, "to the left, and through the doors."

"Will you come get me when she's - uh - decent?"

The nurse nodded. "We'll come get you." She pulled the curtain on Tim's gawking face and returned her attention to Casey. She pulled up a chair and sat. In a low voice, she asked, "Ms. Adams, are you being or have you been abused?"

Casey shifted, uncomfortable on the exam table with its crinkly white paper. *Does she somehow suspect? Does she even know my mom?*

Fidgeting under the nurse's scrutiny, Casey searched for a plausible lie. *I have to say something.*

"No, I fell back and hit my head in the kitchen." She haltingly formed the fabrication.

The nurse touched Casey's hand. Casey jumped a bit.

The nurse's eyebrows rose. "Honey, you're safe here. He can't hurt you."

"See, I'm really clumsy. Wait. He?"

The nurse's eyes widened with compassion. "We see it here all the time, so you don't have to be afraid. We can call a social worker and be certain you're safe."

Casey blinked. *What's she saying?* "I don't understand. Who do you think hit me?"

The nurse stole a glance at the curtain.

"Wait, you don't think Tim - No! He came to help me after..." Casey's words died in her clenched throat. *Shoot. I almost said, 'after Mom hit me.'* The paper beneath Casey crumpled as she rocked. *No matter what I say, I'll get Mom in trouble, I bet.* She hummed to herself to help calm her thoughts. *Or Tim.* Her happy song vibrated in her throat and harkened back to safety and comfort. *I can't believe I've put Tim under suspicion.*

"Honey, Casey," the nurse stopped short of touching her, "I don't mean to upset you. I need you to understand we're here to help. That's all." She pulled out a green hospital gown from the bank of drawers in the exam room. "Put this on, please. You can leave your underthings on, but everything else comes off. Even your socks. We have these slip-resistant socks for you to wear. Okay?"

Casey nodded without looking up.

The nurse made notes on Casey's chart.

Wonder what she's writing?

"I'll be back in a couple of minutes to take your blood pressure. By the way, are you or is there any chance you are pregnant?"

Casey blushed and studied her lap. "Um, no."

"Okay. We'll need a urine sample, though, so when you need to pee, here's a sample cup, wipes, and instructions. The restroom is across from the nurse's station."

"Okay. Can Tim come back once I'm situated, please?"

Silence stretched for a few eternal seconds, but the nurse said, "Of course. He can sit with you until the doctor gives you orders. You'll probably need x-rays and maybe stitches." The nurse flipped a page on the chart. "By the way, when was your last tetanus shot?"

"I-I don't remember."

"Don't worry about it. Change into the gown. The doctor will see you soon."

"And you'll get Tim?"

"As soon as you're ready." She smiled as she pulled the curtain shut behind her.

CHAPTER TEN:
DATE WITH A DOCTOR

Why are hospital gowns open in the back, anyway?
Casey held the flaps with one hand rather than trust
the flimsy ties. *Nobody here needs to see my behind.*
With the other, she held the ruined tea towel to her
head. *And I'm positive gown is not the right term for
this flimsy piece of cloth.* She followed the instructions
for the required sample and took it to the nurse's
station. "Can you get my - uh - Tim now, please?"

A scrub-dressed man nodded. "I'll send him to
you."

Casey made awkward progress to her exam area.
Before she disappeared behind the curtain of her exam
room, a man across the hall "psst'ed" to gain her
attention. The world swayed a bit until Casey found
the source of the summons. Blackness clouded the
man's lower torso. His skin shone a waxy yellow
beneath the unflattering lights. Casey knew before
making eye contact. The man would die before the
night concluded.

Tears stung and fell. She covered her face when
sobs racked her. The tea towel and impromptu ice

pack splatted to the linoleum.

"What's wrong, Miss?" The dying man rested a hand on Casey's shoulder. "I'm Dr. Ohr. Can I help?"

He's dying, but he's still trying to help others. A moan bubbled up in her throat, but she pushed it down until her stomach bounced with hiccups. Between sniffs she asked, "Why did you call me, sir?"

He brushed a bloodied strand of her hair behind her ear. "I'm not sure. I think I didn't want you to be afraid." He smiled around teeth set in receded and bloody gums.

Pull yourself together, Casey. This nice man needs you. "That's kind of you, Dr. Ohr. I don't want you to be afraid, either."

The doctor stilled. He removed his glasses and wiped them with the hem of his hospital gown, revealing wasted legs. "I see." He replaced his glasses. "I wondered how long until I met you."

Casey's head jerked up. Tears splayed from her.

"I think I know you. You're the Lady Death, aren't you? Some of my less fortunate patients told me about you." His gaze swept over her. "You're littler than I thought. And younger. Still, we meet at last." He tipped an imaginary hat.

Snot burned in her throat and dripped from her nose. Tears fell unabated.

The man leaned against the frame of his room. "How long do I have?"

Casey allowed her mind to explore the possibilities. "Not more than an hour."

Dr. Ohr blanched. "I think I knew." He wiped his glasses again. "Suppose that's why I called for you. So how does this work?"

Casey closed her eyes and sniffled, her stomach jolting and her shoulders shaking. "I don't know," Casey stammered. "Not really. All I can do is see and cry." She cupped her face with the hands, and her hair curtained her like a golden mourning veil. "I'm supposed to comfort you, I think, but I don't know how." She whispered, "I'm sorry."

He slung an arm around her shoulder and squeezed. "I believe in an afterlife. I've had a full existence, helped some, made mistakes. My faith will see me through, so don't you worry." He patted her shoulder.

He's comforting me. She turned to face him and hugged the dying man. *So weird. I don't mind hugging him, though I usually shy from such displays.* "I don't think you have anything to worry about."

He stretched a smile. "Me, either." He limped to the chair in his examination room and allowed his head to tilt back. His features relaxed, and his eyes slid closed. His breathing grew ragged and his words labored. "I think I understand. Your presence is comforting. I feel at peace." He opened an eye and tipped his head. "Thank you for the help."

He shuddered. Sweat soured his face and chest. He gasped, and his neck arched until his chin pointed toward the ceiling.

"Nurse," Casey screamed. "Please come quick! Dr. Ohr needs you." She stepped back into her room as the staff rushed to the doctor's aid. She climbed atop the crinkling paper of her exam table and curled into a ball of despair.

Hospital staff answer the screeches of Dr. Ohr's monitors. They yelled codes and tried in vain to save him.

Mascara-laced tears stained the knees of her hospital gown by the time Casey felt his spirit pass. Blood trickled a path through her hair. She sniffled. *Wonder where Tim is?*

An orderly joined her, flipping pages of her chart. He addressed her with a dispassionate voice. "Casey Adams?" He glanced up, paused, and returned his attention to the papers on the clipboard. "The doctor needs x-rays. He set the chart aside and wheeled in a blue wheelchair. "Please have a seat."

Numb, Casey complied. She held still while the technician took the x-rays, and sat in the wheelchair for a return to the exam room.

The open curtains around Dr. Ohr's exam room revealed a crew sterilizing the empty space. Casey said another prayer as she passed. *He was so kind.*

The neurologist and two assistants threw back the curtain for Casey's room and pulled up a wheeled stool for the neurologist, Dr. Cephalius. "So, you have a mild concussion, but I believe you already knew that. It's why you're here. That and the cut." He stood and parted Casey's hair with purple-gloved hands.

Casey's nose crinkled. *Antiseptic doesn't make a nice cologne.*

The neurologist snapped. "Dr. Wilson will tend to the wound."

One of the assistants examined Casey's wound. "No allergies, right, Ms. Adams?"

"None that I know of."

Dr. Wilson fiddled with Casey's hair and grabbed a pair of scissors from his pocket. A "snip, snip" sounded, he returned the scissors and took what looked like a nail gun from a metal cart. After a swipe from an ammonia-smelling packet, the gun bit into Casey's head once, twice, three times. Dr. Wilson set the instrument aside. "You'll have to return to have the staples removed."

Casey shied away, smarting. Her voice shook with indignation. "You put staples into my head?"

"The wound gaped too much for glue."

The neurologist left a precaution sheet and a prescription for pain reliever. "You can dress and leave. Have a nice night." The trio pulled the curtain on their retreat.

Casey rinsed the blood from her hair in the little silvery sink and used the hospital gown to dry it. *Probably not the best plan for a cold March night, but I can't stand how the clots tangle.* She gathered her belongings and retraced her steps to join Tim in the waiting room.

He leapt to her side and touched her arms with care as though she might break. A vein throbbed in his temple. "Are you okay? You were gone forever, and I was so worried."

Casey shivered. *They thought he'd hurt me.* She rested her head against his chest, comforted by his warmth.

At the exit, Aunt Hettie, Rachel, and Malcolm nearly ran into them. "Oh, Casey!" Aunt Hettie dropped the children's hands and embraced Casey.

CHAPTER ELEVEN:
SEEING DOUBLE

Malcolm wrapped his chubby arms around Casey's legs, but Rachel hid her face behind a veil of hair. Tim stepped away to allow the family some space.

Something's wrong. "What's going on?"

Aunt Hettie sniffed. "How are you, honey? Are you okay?" She ran a hand along the side of Casey's head, smoothing her tangled and blood-tainted hair.

"Mild concussion. I was about to text you. They just released me." Casey cocked a head at Aunt Hettie's tear-puffed eyes. "I'm okay. Really."

"I'm so glad." Aunt Hettie released her hold on Casey and rested a gentle hand on Malcolm and Rachel's shoulders. She hunched to the level of their ears and said with a calm voice, "Please sit there for a moment."

Rachel peered from behind her hair, "Aunt Hettie, this isn't necessary. Really."

"Please, Rachel." Aunt Hettie pointed.

So this isn't about me. When the kids took seats, Tim joined them. Casey cleared her throat. "What's going on?"

The intake nurse called for "Rachel Adams."

Aunt Hettie jolted. "I'll be right back." She jerked toward the desk. "Come on, Rachel." Aunt Hettie reached for her.

Rachel slumped to Aunt Hettie's hand.

Rachel looks like a beaten dog. Casey gasped. *Did Mom hurt her?* Casey sat in the seat Rachel abandoned. "Malcolm, what happened?"

Without looking at Casey, Malcolm took a plastic toy from his pocket and banged it into the chair arm once, twice, a third time.

She rested her hand atop his. "Are you okay, Malcolm."

Malcolm's jaw clenched. He stared at the floor and swung his legs. Holes at the toes of his sneakers showed a peek of red socks. The tattered shoelaces floated a hare's breath behind his shoe's progress.

Casey's stomach clenched into a painful rock.

A flutter of white caught her attention. A nurse stared at them from the doorway. She blinked, slow as a lizard caught in the cold. Then her head jerked, and her features blurred like art painted on a turpentine-streaked canvas. She changed, still staring, but no longer dark-eyed or dark skinned.

Casey gasped. *Is that the witch from the equinox ceremony?*

The woman's features changed again, this time, reddened as a sunburn.

But she's not in a dream. I'm awake. Aren't I? Casey rubbed the heels of her hands into her eyes and re-looked.

The woman seemed to fill the entire door frame, eyes cold as blue flame, hair pale as moonlight. She smiled sweet, self-depreciation.

Casey gasped. *That looks like me.*

She rustled Malcolm and whispered in his ear, "Do you see that nurse over there?"

Malcolm looked where Casey covertly pointed, then, eyes wide as pie plates, back at Casey. "How'd you do that?"

Casey shivered. *He sees her.*

"She looks like you, Casey."

The Casey-lookalike's grin angled up, a sharp descent to an evil smirk. Her face transformed into an unflattering caricature.

Casey and Malcolm shuddered.

Malcolm turned his face into Casey's shoulder and whispered, "No, she doesn't. She doesn't look like you at all."

Casey hugged him to her, chills racing up her spine.

Malcolm's small body began to shake with sobs. "She hit her, Casey. She hit you, and she hit Rach-Rach."

The Not-Casey nodded with apparent glee.

Casey lifted her brother's tear-slick chin, confused. "Who did, Malcolm? Who hit us?"

Malcolm blinked away his tears, his face pale beneath red blotches. He touched Casey's bandaged head. He dropped his gaze to his stilled feet and mumbled. "Guess you don't want me to talk about it."

"Oh, do you mean..." Casey sought Rachel and Aunt Hettie. They sat at the registration area. Rachel slumped toward the desk, and her hair obscured her features, her bruise. The heat of realization rushed through her. She rested her head against Malcolm's forehead. "Mom. Did Mom hit Rachel, too?"

Malcolm curled into Casey's lap and whimpered until he drifted off.

With a gentle movement, Casey brushed his fine hair from his eyes. *He hasn't sucked his thumb since he was a toddler.*

Aunt Hettie and Rachel followed the nurse to an examination room.

What did you do, Mom?

Through the window, Tim paced, phone to his ear. Two new patients waited treatment, swelling the ranks in the room to twelve, but nowhere in the room did Casey see her double.

CHAPTER TWELVE:
CAMPING AT AUNT HETTIE'S

While they waited for Rachel and Aunt Hettie, Tim and Malcolm dozed, one with a big head on Casey's shoulder, the other curled in her lap.

I remember a cute kid in the "Jerry Maguire" movie saying the human head weighs eight pounds. She shifted, careful not to disturb the sleepers. *I think he was wrong. Feels more like eighteen.*

A car streaked to the entry, four-ways flashing. The driver leaped from their seat and scrambled to open the back seat. The woman waved her arms, frantic, screaming, her face streaming with a storm of grief.

The feeling of impending death overwhelmed her. *That woman's child isn't going to make it.*

Casey pulled her brother closer and cried into Tim's dark curls. Her stomach convulsed, and she moaned, unable to push from her mind the image of the mother holding her blue and bloated baby until her tears cleared it away.

When she came to herself, Tim and Malcolm provided a cocoon of love.

Tim stroked her hair. "Casey, are you okay?"

Malcolm rubbed her arm. "I love you, Casey."

Aunt Hettie and Rachel emerged from the ER, eyes red-rimmed.

Gasping, Casey struggled to control her agitated heart rate. Her forehead ached with bunched eyebrows and throbbing thoughts. *So many tears tonight. I just want to sleep. I can't take any more.*

Casey and the boys stood to exit. Tim and Malcolm held Casey's hands.

"We're going to have a sleepover." Aunt Hettie offered a wobbly smile. "Well, not you, Tim. I'm sorry." A chuckle caught in her throat and threatened to turn into a sob. Or a snort.

Tim squeezed Casey's hand. "Can I be of any other help?"

Casey reached up on tiptoes and kissed Tim's soft lips. The stubble of not shaving scratched. "You've been amazing. Thank you."

He ran his hand down Casey's hair, his gaze boring into hers. "I'd do anything for you."

Casey blinked back tears. "I know."

"Ah, hem." Rachel tapped her foot.

Tim blushed, sheepish. "I guess I'll be going, then, since you've got a sleepover party to plan." He bent and kissed Casey's forehead, hugged Rachel and Aunt Hettie and ruffled Malcolm's hair. *Malcolm didn't protest. Unusual. Maybe Tim's growing on him?*

Aunt Hettie rested a hand on Tim's arm. "Thank you, Tim."

When did her veins grow so pronounced?

Tim shoved his hands into his pockets, a soft blush darkening his cheeks. "My pleasure, Ma'am." His puppy-eyed gaze caused Casey's heart to miss a beat.

"I love Casey, and you all mean the world to me."

His full lips glistened with kisses Casey wanted to claim if they weren't surrounded by family and injured strangers. She licked her own lips and shied away with a blush.

Tim said goodbye again, hugged Casey, and left.

As she exited, Casey scanned the room. *Where'd that look-alike go?* She shuddered. *And why do I feel like someone's watching me?*

CHAPTER THIRTEEN:
SLEEPOVER WITH LITTLE SLEEP

Aunt Hettie's small apartment shrunk with their arrival. She pulled out a sofa bed for them to share. To open it, they slid her coffee table and its contents into the corner of the room. The metal bed frame scraped it when opened. A narrow walkway allowed them access to the single bathroom and tiny kitchen.

"I'll pick up some milk in the morning. And cereal. Just let me know what you kids like to eat. I don't care how sugary." Aunt Hettie ruffled Malcolm's hair until it stood on end. He smoothed it with a scowl. "How about some chamomile tea before sleep, though?" Aunt Hettie used a lighter to ignite the gas stove beneath her chipped kettle. "I have enough extra toothbrushes in the cupboard. Dentist gives me a new one even when my old one's in good shape, so that worked out." She hunted for four mugs and pulled a teddy bear shaped bottle of honey from her pantry.

Rachel flopped onto the sofa bed. It squeaked and jiggled. She frowned, arms stretched out like a martyr on a cross. "What about clothes? We can't wear these stinky things to bed. And what about tomorrow?"

Aunt Hettie chewed the inside of her cheek. "For tonight, you all can wear my t-shirts. Casey, you'll fit into my clothes." She squinted at Rachel. "I'll have to figure out something for you and Malcolm for tomorrow, though."

Rachel sat up. "Why can't we go get our own clothes?"

The kettle screamed. Aunt Hettie rushed to the cupboard, claimed mugs, and set tea bags to steep. Her voice sounded deflated as a balloon left out on a summer afternoon. "I'll see what I can do. For now, have some tea and get settled."

With an apartment so small, everything remained in easy reach. From their nighttime perch, the kids could reach the living room light or stretch to grab their tea from the kitchen counter.

Two steps took Casey to the front door. Five found her in the bathroom. Another three and she reached Aunt Hettie's bedroom. Casey paced and retraced.

"Casey, honey," Aunt Hettie smiled into her face. "Why don't you get some rest? Rachel's already asleep, and your brother's dead on his feet."

Malcolm startled. "I'm alive, not dead, Aunt Hettie."

She knelt before the kindergartener. "It is just an expression, my dear. An idiom that means you're super tired."

He rubbed his eyes and around a yawn said, "I'm not tired."

Aunt Hettie tucked blankets around Rachel and Malcolm. "Well, keep the bed warm until Casey climbs in, okay?" She kissed them. "And say your prayers."

Malcolm nodded. "Don't be long, Casey, and don't hum. You always hum when you're upset, and you are humming now."

Casey stilled. *Good heavens! He's right. I am humming again.* "Sorry, Malcolm Man."

He nestled into the couch pillow, eyes closed. "It's okay, but stop rocking, too."

She stiffened her muscles to stop mid-sway. *Darn it. I'm a mess.*

Aunt Hettie set a stack of mismatched towels and washcloths on the counter. "Use whatever you need, darling. I'm sorry the place's so small."

"It's wonderful, Aunt Hettie. Thank you for letting us stay tonight."

Aunt Hettie's face took on a pinched look, as though she'd swallowed a lime whole. She slumped into the single kitchen chair beside the counter and whispered, "I can't let you kids go back there, Casey. Not until your mom gets the help she needs."

Casey's eyes slid shut. *We can't stay here for long, though.* "I'll call tomorrow morning and see if Tim can give me a ride to pick up my car and a few things to make the kids more comfortable."

"Only if Tim goes with you, or you wait for me. Honey, your Mom needs help. I never dreamed she'd hurt you girls." Her voice trailed off, and tears slid from her eyes to take the place of all she meant to say.

Casey heard herself hum and stopped.

Aunt Hettie's head hung and her voice came from behind clenched fists. "Rachel wouldn't tell the doctors what happened. Said she fell. That she hurt herself." She peeked between her wrists. "Bet you didn't say anything either." She ran her hands through her graying hair. "Protecting your mom, even though she should be protecting you." She shook her head. "Get some sleep, beautiful girl. I work early shift tomorrow, but don't forget what I said. Don't go over there without either Tim or me, and don't take the kids. Promise?"

Casey straightened the towels into a tidy tower. "Okay."

"I love you, Casey."

Casey nodded. "I love you, too."

After Aunt Hettie had settled into her bed, Casey climbed in beside Malcolm, careful with her weight shifts. *Don't want to wake them.*

Sleep settled over her like a comforter, but before she drifted off, someone knocked on the front door. Three sharp raps. *Who would that be this late at night?* She tiptoed to the door and its peep hole. Nobody stood on the welcome mat.

She returned to her makeshift bed, but again, just as she drifted off, another trio of knocks disturbed her. Nobody on the welcome mat. The clock read 3:36 when she nestled in for the third time that evening, but as before, three loud raps on the door disturbed her. Again, when she peeked out, she saw nobody.

When she stumbled back to bed where Malcolm pawed her, frantic in a nightmare, she soothed him until his breathing calmed.

She slipped into an uneasy dream. Faces blurred like images in rain-streaked windows. Haunting music threaded through indecipherable whispers. She startled awake, chilled, certain someone had called her. Her heart pounded, but the only sounds were street noises and the tick-tick of Aunt Hettie's refrigerator.

I have to get some sleep. She tried to nestle onto the

edge of the sofa bed, but the metal frame bit through the thin mattress, and the kids rustled. *Shoot, don't want to wake them.* With care, she tugged a couch cushion from beneath Malcolm and curled up on the floor. Even through the pillow, she heard rustling downstairs. *Guess the neighbor down there is restless.* Dull aches throughout her body and especially a pounding in her head kept her awake.

She grabbed her phone. *He'll sleep through a text notification, I'm sure.* "Thanks again for the help today. You really are my Superman." *Somehow, just knowing Tim'll read that makes me feel better.*

She blanketed herself with thoughts of his embraces and kisses until she no longer shivered. Sleep continued to elude her, though, and when she at last drifted off, Aunt Hettie's quiet rustles in the kitchen woke her. Coffee brewed, aromatic and noisy, and Casey rose to joined Aunt Hettie for a cup.

Aunt Hettie's bedraggled hair and blood-shot eyes told the tale. *Aunt Hettie mustn't have slept well, either.*

Aunt Hettie took a long sip of her coffee. "I know this won't work for long, but I'll look for a bigger apartment today. You kids will have a safe home. Don't you worry."

"Aunt Hettie," Casey checked that her whisper didn't disturb Rachel or Malcolm. "I was looking into a dorm. Would you rather I stick around? You know, to help out?"

Aunt Hettie rubbed her temple and closed her eyes. "That's not necessary. I can find a bigger place. One closer to the school, maybe, so the kids can walk." She rested her cheek against the warm coffee mug. "You should get a place on campus. I've been saying that since last semester."

Casey felt a bit queasy. *I need to know, but I don't want to ask.* She allowed another sip of bitter caffeine to warm her throat. "What happened, Aunt Hettie? Yesterday. What happened with Rachel?"

"Your mother hit her. Hard. Not to belabor the point, but until she gets right, you kids need a safe place."

Casey's head throbbed where the chair had impacted. *I didn't think she'd get violent with us.* The kids rustled closer on the couch bed, arms clasped around one another. *Or at least not with them.* "We appreciate it, Aunt Hettie. I'll talk to the school. See if they can hold the dorm room. At least until you find a bigger apartment."

"No." Aunt Hettie's thin-fingered grip encircled Casey's, squeezing them into the warm ceramic. "Get your apartment. Honestly, it will be one less person to try to cram into a small space. And if we need you, we can call. Okay?"

As if on cue, Casey's phone alerted for a text. Tim. "You know if you ever need me, I'm your man."

My man. She rested the phone against her bosom a moment with a secretive smile. *Mine.*

Another jingle. Another text. "Do you need a ride to your house? I can be there in fifteen."

He's so thoughtful. "Please, but make it a half hour." She sent the address.

"K." Sent with a heart emoji. She ran her finger along its edges.

"Thank you." Casey's finger hovered over her heart button. With a quick push, she sent one.

CHAPTER FOURTEEN:
TURN TO FACE THE BEAST

After she assured Aunt Hettie she'd be safe when she hurried home to collect clothes and necessities for the kids, Casey pulled on a parka and skipped downstairs to meet Tim.

"Hey, gorgeous!" He scooped her into a tight hug and kissed her. "Your hair's still damp. You'll catch a chill. Hurry. Let's get into the car. I've got the heater pumping."

She blushed. "I rushed the blow drying."

He held the car door for her. "You didn't need to rush, Silly."

"But I do. I've got to be back before Aunt Hettie leaves for work. And I have to get the kids' things for school."

Tim slid the car into gear, his jaw working as though holding back thoughts. They traveled with the classical music station as company for several blocks before he cleared his throat. "How's your cute noggin feeling?"

She shrugged. "It hurts a bit."

He grabbed her hand. "I don't mean to be rude, but

is it safe for you? I mean," He squeezed the steering wheel with his left hand until his knuckles whitened, "I'll go in. I can get whatever you need. Just tell me where to get it." He swallowed. "I don't want you hurt again, Case."

Her head throbbed. "I should be all right. Thanks, though."

When they pulled up to the house, menace seemed to peek from behind the curtains. *She wouldn't hit me again. At least not with a witness.* "Want to meet my crazy mother? She'll probably want to impress you. She likes handsome men."

His expression grew thoughtful. "You want me to distract her while you get what you need?"

"Exactly." She leaned across the gear shift and kissed him. "You're so smart."

He caught her face before she retreated to her seat and kissed her until her knees felt weak. He rested his forehead against hers, hands warm against her cheeks, fingers playing in her hair. "I love you."

She kissed his nose. "I love you, too." With reluctance, she turned to face the beast. *Not really a beast, right? Just a disturbed Mom.* Her stomach lurched. *And my own fear.*

As the car door shut, something caught Casey's eye, a subtle movement from her bedroom.

Wonder if she's up there, snooping around? Not that I have much to snoop through.

Tim took Casey's arm and looped it over the crook of his. He patted her hand. "We've got this." He flashed an engaging smile, one sure to win over any girl, or any crazy Mom. Casey's heart gave a funny thump.

The storm door screeched as they entered. They

stomped the slush from their boots on the kitchen mat before tracking across the kitchen.

"Mom?" Casey's voice trembled.

A weak voice sounded from the darkened living room. "I'm here." Drawn drapes added to the gloom. Mom sprawled across the couch cushions like a Grecian painting, plump arm draped artfully across her eyes. Her rich, velvet robe puddled about her ankles. Chipped toenail polish and the squalor of discarded plates and chip bags did little to change the regal impression. "Casey, darling," she raised herself to an elbow. Her robe slid open, revealing long, thick legs. "Who have you brought to see me?"

This is going just the way I thought it would. "Mom, this is Tim, my boyfriend." Casey stole a sideways glance through a veil of her hair to gage Tim's reaction.

He smiled, calm and collected, and extended his hand. "Nice to meet you, Mrs. Adams. You've raised an amazing woman."

Mom's jaw tightened, but she stretched a smile. "Charmed." She left her hand limp, as though expecting him to bow and kiss her ring.

To her apparent displeasure, he shook it.

Mom patted the couch cushion beside her. "Tell me about yourself, Tim."

Casey caught a quick smirk pull at Tim's mouth.

"Mom, I'm going to run up to my room for a minute. Be right back, okay?"

Mom waved a dismissal as she tucked her feet up under herself to study Tim's chiseled profile.

Casey took the stairs two at a time. First, Rachel's room. She gathered clothes, schoolbooks, an extra pillow - anything she could pack into the overnight bag. She included toys for Malcolm when she packed his bag.

Something shuffled in the hallway as she tossed the last of her schoolbooks into her backpack. Casey peeked around the doorframe but saw nothing unusual. Chills crept up her spine. Better hurry, just in case. She hefted the bags down the back staircase and out the back door to load them in Tim's car. When she turned to return to the house and rescue Tim, something moved behind her curtains. The quick glimpse of a pale face disappeared before Casey could identify its owner. Too small to be Mom or Tim, though. Dad's not home. What the...?

Casey chewed the inside of her cheek, indecisive. Should I rescue Tim or see who the heck's in my room? A cold breeze rifled through her hair, and her chills intensified. Tim'll be okay for a few minutes. She crept up the back stairs to surprise the interloper.

The air felt icy. Did someone open a window, or is Mom playing with the thermostat again? Casey hugged herself for warmth as she tiptoed to her room. No windows open. No strangers. Nothing out of place. She stalked to the hallway, silent and slow.

Something flitted by, the merest glimpse of a pale woman wearing white.

Casey dodged back behind her door, startled. Her heart hammered. That wasn't Mom or Tim. Who's in my house?

With a deep breath, Casey mustered her courage and dashed into the hallway to confront the stranger. "Who's there?" she yelled like a sentry in an old castle. Her breath puffed before her face, but nobody answered. The empty hallway chilled her. She forced her trembling knees toward the closed bathroom door. "Show yourself. Or I'll call the police!"

Tim called from the foot of the stairs, worry plain upon his face. "Casey, are you okay?"

Casey leaned over the railing and stage-whispered, "Tim, somebody's up here! I think she's hiding in the bathroom." She pointed.

In a flash, Tim reached her side. He ran warm hands along her shoulders and whispered, "Do you think it's an intruder?"

Casey nodded, fortified by his presence.

"Stay here. I'll check it out."

Casey bristled. "No, I'm coming."

Tim closed his eyes as though summoning patience. "You are stubborn. You know that, right?"

Casey nodded.

They crept to the door. Tim put a hand on the knob and held up three fingers, then two, and at one he flung the door wide.

Casey's white nightgown, one so like the one their friend Ryan had painted her wearing and that she had never worn since, fluttered from over head to the tiled floor. They pushed back the shower curtain and opened the linen closet door. Nobody lurked in the corners. Nobody jumped out at them. Only the nightgown remained out of place.

Casey retrieved it, her hands numbed by the cold flannel. "Where did this fall from?" Her nose wrinkled. "Ew, it stinks!" I've smelled this before. Like a rot or decay. When? Where?

Casey held it away from her and dropped it into the laundry basket.

Tim rubbed his nose and turned to check the

hallway and rooms. "I don't see anyone, Casey. Are you sure there was a person, and not something hanging from, maybe the shower curtain rod that tricked your eye?"

Casey shook her head. "No, I saw a woman in the hallway. She breezed by. I'm positive." *Or at least I think I'm positive.*

Tim took her hands. "Gosh, you're frozen." He kissed her fingertips and gently rubbed her hands. He lowered his voice. "Could it have been a vision? You know, like at the hospital?"

"No, this was different." It wasn't only Tim's nearness that warmed her. The temperature had returned to normal. *I think whoever that was, left.* She placed a hand on his. "I have what we need in the car. Let's get the heck out of here. I've had enough fun at home for a while."

As though on cue, her mother called in a sing-song voice, "You two aren't up to any hanky-panky, are you?"

"No, Mom." Casey pulled away from Tim. "Geeze." She grabbed a book from her shelf, closed the bedroom doors, and sighed. "Let's go."

"Okay. But just so you know," he whispered into her ear, "I'm not opposed to some hanky-panky with you." His warm breath tickled.

Casey pushed away. "Stop. She'll hear." As they made their way downstairs, Casey shivered, but not with cold or dread. A little hanky-panky might be nice with Tim. Heat rose in her cheeks, so she pulled her hair forward and tipped her head down. "See you, Mom. Tim and I are off to school."

She placed a hand to her chest, fingertips resting

delicately on her collarbone, and used a girlish voice. "School? I thought you graduated, Casey. Last year."

Casey sighed. Always the same schtick. "College, Mom. Remember?"

"College?" She blinked, incredulous. "Really?" She turned her gaze and sidled to Tim. She marched manicured fingernails along Tim's arm. "So you're a college boy, are you?"

Tim stepped closer to Casey and slid an arm around her shoulders. "Yes, Ma'am. Ol' Nor'Eastern, Just like Casey." He gave Casey's shoulder a squeeze. "Well, it was really nice meeting you." He nodded to Mrs. Adams. "Please give my best to Mr. Adams."

Mom tilted her head, coy as a soap opera star. "You be sure to come by and visit me anytime you want. You hear me?"

Tim nodded and squeezed a bit more on Casey's shoulders. "Thank you, Ma'am. Well, good day, now."

Tim nearly closed Casey's coat in the car door in his haste to leave.

CHAPTER FIFTEEN: NOWHERE TO HIDE

Once they reached the highway, Tim released a gust of breath. "That was interesting."

Casey wrung her hands. *Now he'll break up with me. He's met my crazy mother, and I was seeing things.* She stole a glance at his handsome profile. Her gaze lingered on his full lips. *He probably thinks I'm crazy, too.* She rocked forward and back until the seat belt tightened. *Maybe I am crazy.* She licked her lips, remembering Tim's latest kiss. *I don't want him to break up with me!*

The urgency inside burst in a desperate slew. "I'm so sorry. I told you, my mother's a bit off. Well, more than a bit. Certifiable. Really. But she busted out of the institution. They couldn't hold her, I guess, and now she's not taking medicine because she said she doesn't like how it makes her feel. I can't believe she hit on you like that! I mean, I was right there! Of course, you're so good looking, of course anyone would want to hit on you. But. Ew. Who wants my mother hitting on them?" Her face burned and she choked out, "Unless you liked her, you know, hitting on you."

She swallowed. "But I hope not. Because that's creepy. And besides, I don't want you to want anyone else."

What the heck am I doing? Shut up, Casey! The heat spread across her face to include her neck. Her body strained against the restraint, anxious to become a comforting pendulum.

Tim rested his hand on her knee. "I don't."

His touch calmed her racing heart, and tension eased from her shoulders and stomach. "You don't what?"

"I don't want anyone but you. Not a supermodel or a famous actress. Not a cheerleader or even Miss America."

Her anxiety melted beneath his dark-eyed gaze.

He bobbed his head, jaw tight. "I want you, Casey Adams, and I hope you don't think I'm a fool for telling you. I need you to understand." His smile softened the rugged planes of his face. "You make me think of forever in a whole new way." His stare intensified. "I can't imagine my life without you."

Casey swallowed around the lump in her throat. Her voice puffed, breezy with relief. "You don't think I'm crazy?"

He chuckled. "Well, maybe a little. But I like your kind of crazy." He squeezed her knee.

Tears welled. "I'm sorry my life is so complicated." The seatbelt held her against the seat, locked and abrasive.

"It's not your fault. You have one hell of a lot to deal with, and to be honest, I can't think of anyone else strong enough to take all that you endure. You're amazing."

Tim pulled into a spot outside Aunt Hettie's and

put the car in park. He turned to her. "Casey, I love you."

Casey pushed the release on the seatbelt and leaped to drape herself in his arms. "I love you, too, Tim!"

Their kisses grew in passion. His hands sought the shelter beneath her blouse, and she gasped and jerked away. *Too much!* When she pulled from his embrace, she bumped the car's horn. It blasted a brash proclamation.

Tim, color high in his cheeks, laughed. "Guess they know we're here now." His eyes lingered on her unzipped coat and askew blouse. "Suppose we should head in." His nostrils flared and the rise and fall of his chest slowed as he collected the suitcases.

Casey struggled to calm her breathing as she adjusted her clothing. Where his hand touched ached with remembrance.

Before they knocked on Aunt Hettie's door, Casey cleared her throat. "Tim." She couldn't make eye contact. Despite the nippy weather, her skin burned. "I'm sorry. I want to, you know…"

He cupped her chin and forced her to look into his intense gaze. "When you're ready, it will be like fireworks." He kissed her forehead, "A beautiful," her cheek, "perfect," her other cheek, "amazing," His lips lingered a breath from hers. "conflagration."

Their hug supported one another, pillars fallen together in a precarious new configuration, until Aunt Hettie's door swung open unbidden.

Rachel smirked. The bruising around her eyes did nothing to diminish the impishness of the expression. "Welcome back, Lovebirds."

"Stop harassing them, Rachel." With a knowing smile, Aunt Hettie pulled Rachel inside. She grabbed a suitcase. "Let me get that." She hefted the bag inside and placed it on the closed sofa bed. "You two, get dressed for school. I can't get you there late or your teachers will have my hide."

Malcolm's eyebrows lowered with confusion. "You want to play hide and seek, Aunt Hettie?"

Aunt Hettie chuckled. "No, hide as in my skin. So let's not be tardy."

Malcolm shook his head and selected an outfit. "My teacher doesn't take people's skin. That would be yucky. What would she do with it, anyway? You're a lot shorter than she is, Aunt Hettie."

"Malcolm, that's another idiom. You know, like we talked about before. Aunt Hettie means the teachers will be upset with her if you're late. So please hurry."

"English doesn't make sense," he grumbled as he toddled into the bathroom to change. Rachel claimed Aunt Hettie's room, and they both were quick to be ready.

Casey had their book bags situated, and Aunt Hettie made their lunches.

Aunt Hettie pulled a knitted cap over Malcolm's ears. "So Malcolm, here's a new phrase for you. We're off to the races." She swatted his bottom with a fond chuckle. "Now head out to the car. Zipper up, will you? It's not summer yet."

"Off to the races?" Malcolm repeated as he trudged with Rachel to Aunt Hettie's car.

"Honestly, Malcolm," Rachel huffed with pre-teen irritability.

Aunt Hettie locked the door and smiled after them.

"You three are such good kids." She pecked Casey on the cheek and gave Tim a quick hug. "I don't know. You might be a good kid, too. What do you think, Casey? Is Tim a good guy?"

Casey smiled. "Absolutely."

"Well then, if Casey said it's so, then it is so." She waved goodbye and dashed to her car. "Have a good day. Oh, and Casey, let me know how the housing works out." She paused outside the driver's side door. The keys jangled from her grip. "Do you think you can move in today? That would be ideal if so."

Casey struggled to interpret the meaning of Aunt Hettie's words. Sometimes she couldn't understand subtleties. With Aunt Hettie, Casey decided upon levity. "Trying to get rid of me, are you?"

Aunt Hettie laughed. "Of course not. I'm betting you'll be more comfortable in a dorm room is all. I don't think you slept much on my couch last night, especially since I found you on the floor in the morning." She waved again, got into the car, and pulled away.

"Shall we?" Tim opened the passenger side door as though he were a footman and she Cinderella entering a carriage on the way to a ball. She stepped inside and wondered what dancing with Tim would be like. His body close, warm, and strong, guiding her across a parquet floor.

Before he took his seat on the driver's side, her blush burned bright.

CHAPTER SIXTEEN:
SOMEWHERE TO RUN

"Ms. Adams, I'm thrilled to inform you of the availability of a housing stipend. You're welcome to move in whenever you're ready. Your roommate, Ms. Deirdre Lowry, is already ensconced in the room and anticipates your arrival." Mr. Kean extended his hand.

Casey's head spun. Nothing ever worked out so easily for her. "Thank you so much." She bobbed her head and gripped her stuffed overnight bag with both hands, eager to ignore his handshake. "I'll get out of your hair." *Malcolm would like that phrase, I bet, especially since Mr. Kean hasn't any hair.* She stifled a private giggle and dashed to her new home in Women's Dormitory West.

Outside the door, she paused. *Do I knock? I mean, it's supposed to be my room, too, now.*

Someone cleared their throat behind her. "Are you going in or what? Loitering in the hall like this seems kind of stupid."

Casey spun to find Deirdre Lowry behind her. "Hi Deirdre. I, um, didn't know if I should knock."

Deirdre shook her head and brushed past Casey to

open the door and step inside. She flopped onto the made bed, face first, arms splayed. Muffled by the pillow, her voice sounded husky. "That's your bed, of course. The fridge is mine, but if you want to use it, you can. Just don't take up all the space or eat my food."

"Sounds fair." Casey set her meagre belongings on the mattress and plopped beside them. *Guess I need a sheet and comforter. And a pillow.*

Deidre remained prone and face down. Beneath her bed, the pink tote held the scavenged pills.

Hope I can somehow encourage her to get rid of them.

Silence stretched as the sun rose. *This is getting awkward, even for me.* As Casey rocked, the bed made little creaking complaints.

She studied the ceiling, hoping for conversation starter help. *Wonder how those marks got up there?* She quelled the queasy feeling and forced out words. "Looks like someone walked up there." She pointed upward. "See? Footprints."

Deirdre barrel rolled until she faced where Casey indicated. "Someone probably threw their shoe up which scuffed the paint."

Casey nodded. "That's good thinking. Makes sense." Casey envisioned bored students tossing shoes. "Bet it annoyed whoever was in the room above here." She giggled as she imagined the irregular pitter-patter.

Deirdre turned her cheek into the pillow to face Casey, her expression unfathomable. "Want to find out?"

Casey's mouth fell open. "What do you mean?

Throw our shoes?"

Deirdre shrugged. "Yeah." She brought her leg to her chest and removed the sneaker. She gave it a heft. It soared up to the ceiling and redoubled its pace on descent. Deirdre caught it just before it slammed into her face. "No scuff. Maybe it depends on the shoe. Try yours."

Casey contemplated. *I could get into trouble with whoever's upstairs, but this might be a way to make Deirdre a friend.* She untied her shoe and threw. If fell short of the intended, and Casey missed the catch. Casey gasped. "Now the people downstairs will be wondering what's going on."

"You worry too much. Try again."

Might as well. Casey threw harder, and the shoe grazed the ceiling. "There's a scuff!"

"Now we've left a mark of our own."

Casey nodded.

CHAPTER SEVENTEEN:
TIME CHANGES

Casey sat beside Jaimie in Dr. Bridges' psychology class.

Jaimie reached across and hugged her friend. "Are you a neighbor now?"

Casey nodded. "Is your roommate settled in?"

"Uh huh." Jaimie's head bob sent a riot of curls tumbling over her thin shoulders. "She's pretty cool. She's meeting us after class for coffee, k?"

"Um..."

Dr. Bridges' cleared throat ended their conversation and began the class, but Casey couldn't concentrate.

Coffee after psychology is our thing, Jaimie's and mine. Why's Amber coming along?

Dr. Bridges closed his notebook with a thump of dismissal.

Casey sat up straight, surprised into alertness. *Shoot, I missed the whole class!*

Jaimie stuffed her backpack with her customary speediness and almost skipped from the lecture hall before Casey had her things gathered.

"Hey, wait up!" Disused to shouting, Casey's voice

did not carry beyond her desk. Casey patted her books into place and zippered the backpack, her heart pounding. *Everything is cattywampus! I hope my papers aren't crinkled.* She fought the impulse to check on the state of her pack as Jaimie's slight form disappeared into the mass of psych students. *Why's Jaimie in such a hurry?*

She ignored a nagging stitch in her side to reach her friend.

Jaimie smiled. "Where were you? I thought you were right behind me."

Casey gulped for breath. "What's the hurry?"

"Amber's class is closer to the coffee shop, and I didn't want her to wait. You know, worry that she'd be stood up or something."

Casey calmed her heart rate. In through the nose, out through the mouth. *Glad I don't have asthma or something. Running like this would aggravate it, I bet.*

The coffee shop bustled with warm energy.

Jaimie spread her arms wide to embrace her new roommate. "There you are! I hope you didn't wait long?"

Amber glowed with the attention. "Not long at all. I grabbed a table and some drinks." She pointed to a raised circular table with two tall, wire-framed chairs and two steaming mugs.

"Oh," Jaimie's gaze flicked to Casey, and a deep red stained her cheeks. Her voice deepened from the frantic excitement of greeting to a cowed alto. "That's sweet, Amber, but we need a table for three." Jaimie looped her thin arm through Casey's. "Remember, I told you we're meeting my bestie here."

Amber's blush rivaled Jaimie's. "Oh, I'm sorry," she

stammered. "I misunderstood."

Casey patted Jaimie's hand and extricated herself. "It's okay. I'll get a cup."

Casey joined the queue of caffeine hopefuls while Jaimie and Amber climbed atop the raised seats. They put their heads together, conspirators unaware or unconcerned about Casey's feelings of ostracism. Students occupied all the other tables in the Brew Two, and no extra chairs littered the place.

When she reached the counter, Casey fumbled with her wallet.

The harassed barista's smile wobbled. "Must be Monday, huh?" He brushed the front of his green apron and thrust out his chest. The name tag read Simon. "Do you want your usual?"

Taken aback, Casey nodded. "Um, sure." *Usual? Do I always get the same drinks?* She considered. *Other than pumpkin spice in the fall, I guess I do.*

"Great! One medium vanilla caramel latte coming right up." Simon typed the order into the cash register.

I suppose I'm not a terribly adventurous diner. Or drinker. She counted out and handed her payment. *Still, why'd he know my drink?*

With a start, she realized he didn't ask her name. "Oh, by the way, please put it under Casey."

Simon tilted his head and considered her from behind his mop of shiny hair. He chuckled. "I know. Casey Adams." He peeked around the crowd. "Where's your friend? Jaimie, right?"

Her gaze skimmed his features. *Yeah, I think he's usually here when Jaimie and I visit.* She tipped her head toward Jaimie and Amber.

His smile as he handed her change erased some of

the strain and tiredness from his young face. "Thanks for your continued patronage."

Casey forced herself to meet his gaze. "Thank you."

"You're welcome."

Casey studied the edge of the counter as she sidled to the retrieval area. *Why does Simon remember me and my drink, but my best friend seems to have forgotten me?*

As though hearing Casey's thoughts, Jaimie turned and waved.

Casey dipped her head. *I should be ashamed of myself. Amber seems like a nice girl, and I should be happy for Jaimie, not jealous.*

The preparation barista called her name, and Casey retrieved her drink. Its spicy aroma wafted as she made her way gingerly through the crush of people. *It's not usually this busy here.*

Jaimie and Amber hopped from the elevated chairs when she reached them.

Jaimie rested a hand on Casey's back. "Let's walk. What do you say, girlfriend? It's way too crowded here today."

Casey smiled gratitude. She followed in Jamie's wake. Outside, an assault of chilled air washed over them. Casey tightened her grip around the warmth of her coffee cup.

"Casey, Mimi tells me you're in my old dorm room. How's that working out for you?"

Casey furrowed her brow. "Mimi?"

Jaimie danced in a small circle. "That's Amber's nickname for me. Cute, huh?" She skipped to a trash bin. Her coffee cup made a ringing thump when she banked it. She tipped her head skyward and closed her eyes. "It feels so different from who I've always been. Kind of a nice break."

Casey shrugged. "If you like it."

Amber's empty cup followed Jaimie's into the bin. "Mimi suits you. Besides, you didn't like it when I called you James."

Casey jolted. *Of course she didn't like being called her dead twin's name.*

Jaimie paled but gave no explanation.

Amber checked her phone. "Listen, we'd better hurry or we'll be late for Magnus's Sociology class. Don't want to upset her. She's got that fiery French temper."

Jaimie and Amber laughed, bodies drawn together in mirth as they intoned, "Zees is not acceptable!"

Maybe I should have asked Deirdre to join us? Heck, I couldn't if I wanted. I don't have her cell number. She scowled at her phone. *What kind of friend am I?*

Jaimie wrapped an arm around Amber's waist. "I've heard tales, but she's such a nice lady. I have a hard time justifying the rumors with my experiences." The women proceeded along the cobblestone pathway toward their lecture hall, giggling like younger girls.

Casey fell behind, a lonely ache her companion. *I take it they have Sociology together.*

Jaimie spun to face her. "Casey, are you coming?"

Casey shook her head. *Trail along like the proverbial third wheel? No thanks.* "I think I'm going to meet Tim."

Jaimie's mouth fell slack for a moment. She nodded. "Okay. Well, I'm sorry we didn't get to talk as much as usual." She swooped close for a hug.

Before they'd separated, Casey thought, *I miss her*

already.

A chill breeze ruffled Casey's hair and raised gooseflesh along her arms. *Is someone watching me?* A scan of the area revealed nobody, still the feeling of unease persisted.

While they hurried away, Casey sent a text message to Tim. "Hey! What're you doing now? Do you have time to meet?"

His immediate response made her smile. "You know I'm at your disposal as always, milady! Where do you want to meet?"

Casey suggested a bench between their next classes and made her way there to wait.

Another jingled text message, this one from Jaimie. "How's your head? Didn't want to mention anything in front of Amber. I know you're a private person. Tim told me a little about what happened, but if you want to talk... BTW, you could press charges against her. She had no right, and maybe a little time in prison might straighten her out. I love you Bestie."

The words blurred as tears populated Casey's eyes. She typed, "I love you, too, Jaimie."

She swiped her sweater sleeve across her eyes before Tim arrived.

He kissed her cheek. "How do you do it, Casey?"

"Do what?"

"Take my breath away every damn time I see you?"

She blinked into his chocolatey eyes and sighed. *You take mine, too, but I could never admit that?*

CHAPTER EIGHTEEN:
SIGHTING

They sat in amiable silence for a while, Tim cradling Casey's hand, both consumed by internal considerations, oblivious to spring blossoming around them until a bird landed on Casey's knee.

She gasped but remained still.

Its tiny claws gripped her denim jeans as it trilled a song. As fast as its landing, the sparrow spread its wings and fluttered to a low branch in the crabapple beneath which they sat. As a remembrance of the magical experience, Casey found a single brown feather. She ran its quill along her arm.

"You even charm the birds from their nests." Tim traced the path of the quill.

"I need to go home again, Tim. I forgot sheets and stuff for the dorm room. And my car."

Tim swallowed. "I'll go with you. Distraction duty again." He chuckled.

"You don't have to distract, but I could use a

ride. Or I'll take a bus. I think it will be okay at home. I'll breeze in and out." *Breeze, like the chill upstairs, cold as death's breath.* Casey shivered.

"I've been thinking about what you said, Casey. I don't think Jaimie's trying to exclude you. She gets so wrapped up in things, she forgets herself sometimes. I know she loves you."

Casey nodded but gritted her teeth. "I know that." *I needed to express my frustrations and confusion, and I usually vent to Jaimie.*

He pulled at his jacket collar and his eyes shifted. "She had a point, though. You could press charges against your mom."

No, I couldn't. The words strangled in her throat. "I don't want to do that."

Tim rested an arm around her shoulders and squished close. "You always take care of everyone except yourself. I mean, you're watching out for your roommate, your kid brother and sister, your mom, even after she hurt you." He squeezed her shoulder. "I wish you would take care of yourself half as well as you look after others." He lifted her chin toward his face. "Or allow me to take care of you."

Chills raced up her spine, but not from Tim's touch. Casey wheeled from him, certain someone spied on them. She gasped and slipped back into Tim's comforting bulk.

Sheltered beneath the canopy of a copse of skeletal aspen trees, the Casey Double from the hospital grinned, mouth unnatural and eerie, eyes malignant and unblinking.

A flock of red-winged blackbirds swooped through. Its noisy flight arced to obscure the horrible vision, and when the birds landed in other nearby trees, the Casey Double was gone.

Tim's strong arms wrapped around Casey. "Are you okay? You're trembling." He gave her a comforting squeeze. "I didn't know you were afraid of birds."

"I'm not." Casey shrugged from his protection to approach the aspen grove. Tender blades of grass struggled from the packed ground, thin as corpse hairs, except where the apparition had stood. In that spot, frost glistened like a cataract.

Tim touched her shoulder and whispered, "Was it a vision, like," he cleared his throat and lowered his eyes, "when someone dies."

Casey shook her head. "This was something else entirely." She looked into his widened eyes. "You didn't see anything? Somebody standing here, staring at us?" Dread settled over her like a suffocating cloud. *He didn't see it.*

Tim scanned the campus, tense and alert. "Watching us?"

Casey nodded. "Yeah, standing right here."

"Can you describe the person?"

Casey closed her eyes. "Not really." *If I do, you'll think I'm insane.* "But I saw her before, at the hospital."

Tim froze like a hunting dog hot on a scent. "Do you think she's stalking you?"

"I don't know." *Why would she stalk me? And who would want to look like me?*

CHAPTER NINETEEN: INVESTIGATION

Classes went by in a blur of overblown academia. Assignments and essays heaped atop chapters of dry reading. Casey returned to an empty dorm room and deposited her books on the bed designated for her. Deirdre was not back, so Casey used a sheet of lined paper to write a note. "Went home to collect sheets and a pillow. Be back before curfew." She paused, chewing her lips. *Social niceties aren't my strong suit.* "I hope you had a good day." She jotted her cell phone number. "Call or text if you need anything."

Instead of eating lunch at the quad, she and Tim grabbed burgers on the way to collecting her car. At home, Casey's mother snored on the couch. She tiptoed up the backstairs to gather sheets, a pillow, and blankets. She tossed clothes into a fabric bag and hurried outside.

"You got everything?" Tim stole glances at the house, alert as a watchdog.

After giving Tim a "thank you" kiss, Casey sunk into the seat of her car and allowed Beethoven's "Fur Elise" to wash away the feeling of lurking doom. They caravanned to campus. Once there, though, she had to park in the visitor's lot on the far side of campus since she didn't yet have a resident's parking pass.

"Text me when you get to your room." Tim waved.

Casey enjoyed walking in the crisp, spring air. Tiny purple crocus dotted the mud and lingering snow alongside the cobblestone path, cheerful reminders of warmer days to come. The rhythm of her footfalls provided a steady and calming percussion for the jumbled lyrics in her mind. Her phone jingled.

A text from Aunt Hettie. "You're not gonna believe this. CYF at apartment. Said they're taking the kids."

Casey dropped her phone. The car behind her beeped. She reacted too late for the light which slipped from yellow to red. The driver of the car behind her threw frustrated arms in the air.

CYF. Children and Youth Services. Casey's stomach lurched. *Taking the kids? Why?*

The frustrated driver blared his horn as soon as the light changed to green. Casey's tires squealed as she punched the gas harder than usual to accommodate the impatient man and her desire to rush to Aunt Hettie's apartment.

Once there, Aunt Hettie pulled Casey into a crushing embrace. "Thank God you're here." Her red-rimmed eyes puffed to ruddy slits, and her tears washed rivulets in her foundation that dripped onto the starched collar of her waitress uniform.

Malcolm's wavery voice called to her. "Casey."

She fell on one knee and spread her arms wide. "Come here, you."

He ran to her embrace, face pale with worry. He whispered into her ear, "This bad guy said we'd have to go with him until he can figure out who's lying."

Lying? She whispered, "Who do they think is lying."

His chubby little body trembled. "Either Aunt Hettie or," he sniffed, "Momma."

Momma?

"I never said anything of the kind. Now if you'll excuse me," The thin man adjusted the papers on his clipboard. "If you are Casey Adams, I need to speak with you." He glared at Aunt Hettie. "Alone."

Aunt Hettie held out a hand calloused and raw from hard work and cleaning chemicals. "Come on, Malcolm. I'll get you some ice cream."

"No, you won't." The man pinched his lips into a tiny, crinkled line. "Do not leave the property."

Malcolm's nostrils flared. "You made my sister leave here. When will I see Rachel?" He pointed a finger, most of his body hidden behind Aunt Hettie's bony legs. "You better not hurt her. She better not be scared."

The CYF man pinched the bridge of his angular nose. "Malcolm, I already explained to you, my associate and I are here to protect children. To protect you and Rachel. And maybe Casey." He swept her with a pale-eyed glance. "We try to make sure kids like you are not scared or hurt. That's our job."

Malcolm narrowed his eyes, distrustful.

Casey agreed. "Why don't you two go into Aunt Hettie's bedroom and play a card game?"

Aunt Hettie's head bobbed. "That's a great idea. I have a deck from my co-worker's last vacation. They have sea horses on them."

Malcolm's lower lip trembled. "Okay, but I want Rachel back." He pointed again, and the tremble left his lip. "And don't you scare Casey, either."

The man nodded, solemn. "I will do my best."

Once Aunt Hettie and Malcolm were out of eyeshot, the man motioned to a chair. He set his phone beside him and drew out a laptop. "I need to take your statement, Miss Adams."

Casey stopped mid-rock. *Put away your crazy. The kids are counting on you.* She couldn't raise her eyes to meet his penetrating gaze. "What kind of statement?"

He pushed a button on his phone. "I'm recording." He tapped the phone. "Miss Adams, why were you in the hospital recently?"

Casey squirmed. "I hit my head. Got some staples." She touched the crown of her head.

"And how did you hit your head?"

"I'm clumsy."

"I see." He flipped a page on his clipboard. "And your sister, Rachel. Why was she in the hospital?"

Do they suspect Mom? "I'm not sure."

"Miss Adams, you're seventeen, right?"

Sluggish thoughts collided in her overwhelmed mind. *Seventeen? Am I seventeen? I just graduated, so yes, I'm seventeen.* Casey nodded.

"Please answer aloud for the recording."

Casey cleared her throat. "Yes."

"You turn eighteen in July?"

She nodded again.

"Aloud, please."

She flicked a glance at the sharp features of his face. Intelligence and suspicion resided there. "Yes, sir." *What does he want?*

"Do you and your brother Malcolm and your sister Rachel live here with your Aunt Hettie?"

Casey studied the worn and stained carpet. A patch by her foot resembled the black dog she met in the cemetery the other day.

"Am I making you nervous?"

Casey snapped her head up and forced her eyes to steady on the spot between the man's eyebrows. She swallowed a song, one Tim's band covered when they were still performing. "Unforgiven" by Metallica. *Shoot, was I humming?* She nodded. *Out loud, remember?* Her voice sounded thin as the spring fog. "Yes, sir. You do make me nervous."

He set the clipboard down and rested his long-fingered hands atop. "Miss Adams, I am sorry. I didn't even introduce myself." He extended his right hand. "My name's Daniel Killian. I work for Family Services to see to the protection of our county's youth. Although you're almost grown, you're still a youth under my jurisdiction, and," he leaned forward, making his eyes level with her gaze, "even if not, I'd need to interview you on behalf of your siblings. There was a report of the injuries sustained by you and Rachel, and I am here to investigate."

Dread collected within Casey. "Who filed a report?"

"All Childline reports are anonymous."

"What about facing your accuser?"

"Nobody's accusing you of anything, Miss Adams. We are investigating on your behalf."

Casey's skin vibrated, and she longed to rake fingernails deep into the itchy flesh. She calmed her breathing rate. *In - one two three. Out - one, two, three, four, five.* "Who is accused?"

The man settled into his seat, hands still stretched over the papers held in place by an old metal clip. "I'm not at liberty to say."

His fingers imprisoned information, those long, artistic fingers trapping information instead of freeing songs on a piano like Tim's brother Tommy sometimes did. Between the digits, she spotted the words "Childline," "hospital," and "stolen."

"Where is my sister?"

His fingers twitched, revealing a glimpse of another word. It began with HET.

Aunt Hettie.

As though doused with ice water, cold settled into Casey's joints. "Please tell me where you took my sister."

"I'll make a deal with you. After you answer my questions, I promise to give you as much information as I'm allowed. Now, has anyone harmed you?"

Her hand stole to her stapled head. The wound throbbed beneath her palm, as though the blood hummed with truth. Hummed. *I love JS Bach's "Air on the G-String."*

"Miss Adams?"

Casey snapped to the here-and-now. Shoot. She untangled her finger from her hair. *I'm twirling my hair, too. I'm quite a spectacle of myself. Everything I've been taught not to do, I'm doing.* She side-eyed the interviewer. "Sorry. What was the question?"

He reached toward but fell short of touching Casey. "I'm here to help."

She nodded. *Sure you are.*

He didn't blink, and Casey squirmed under his scrutiny. "Miss Adams, do you work?"

Casey nodded.

"Where?"

"At the library. Part time."

"Has anyone there ever made you uncomfortable with a physical touch?"

She crinkled her eyebrows, and the corner of her lips twitched. She worked with calm, neat, quiet bibliophiles. Not one combatant among the lot of them. "No, sir."

"That's good." He made a note on his paper. "What about your boyfriend? I hear you have one. Do you fear he might harm you? Or anyone else?"

Tim, solid, protective, gentle Tim with the kindest eyes. She giggled. "No."

"Has your father ever laid hands on you?"

Casey rankled, her breathing quicker than her heart rate. "No. He'd not hurt a soul." *Does this interviewer ever blink?*

"Casey, has your Aunt Hettie ever harmed you or your brother or sister?"

Casey frowned. She spat the word with vehemence. "Never."

"Why are you living in this little apartment?"

Her eyes swam away from his unflinching consideration. Her voice softened with her lie. "We thought a sleepover party would be fun."

He tapped a pen on the board and looked around the cramped quarters. "So your visit was just for the night?"

"Um..."

Malcolm burst from the bedroom, tears streaming down his flushed cheeks. "Now you stop it right now, Mister! You're upsetting my sister."

Aunt Hettie's chase ended before she entered the room. "I'm sorry. He got away from me. Malcolm, come with me, honey, until Mr. Killian's done talking with Casey."

Mr. Killian waved his hand. "It's fine. He can stay." He pinched his lip and tipped his chin as though to point out Aunt Hettie could not.

She took the hint. "I'm here if you need me." Her bedroom door clicked closed behind her.

Casey untangled her finger from her hair again. "Malcolm, I'm okay. Look at me."

His chest heaved, and his body shook, but he melted into her arms and buried his face in her lap.

He sniffled. "She didn't mean it. She loves us."

The investigator lowered his voice to a calm rumble. "Who didn't mean it, Malcolm? Who hurt your sisters?"

Malcolm whispered into Casey's jeans the truth, but the word did not carry beyond the fibers, and he would not repeat it.

Neither could Casey bring herself to incriminate her mother, despite the pain she caused. Plus, how humiliated would her father feel as a result? Better to keep her thoughts private.

After another half an hour of non-answers, Mr. Killian rubbed his eyes with apparent resignation. "Well, since everything seems to be in order, I'll take you two home."

Malcolm froze in Casey's lap.

Casey counted the stitches along Malcolm's overalls. Their regularity calmed. "No, sir, we were having another sleepover with Aunt Hettie tonight."

A knock at the front door made Casey jump.

Mr. Killian remained still.

Casey bit her lip. "Should I answer that? Or can I

get Aunt Hettie?"

A second round of knocks sounded, impatient. Short staccato echoes of last night's eerie interruptions.

Mr. Killian pushed papers into his satchel. "I suggest you get your Aunt, and we'll be on our way."

Cotton dry, Casey attempted to swallow. "But we're staying here, remember? And we'd like Rachel to come back."

A third knock brought a timid Aunt Hettie from the bedroom. "Should I get that?"

Mr. Killian shoved more papers into his bag and nodded. "Feel free."

Aunt Hettie ran a shaking hand through messy hair and smoothed her uniform before pulling the door open. She gasped and stepped away from the opening.

Two uniformed police officers entered. The shorter of the two removed his hat. "Good afternoon."

Casey suspected it would be anything but a good afternoon.

CHAPTER TWENTY:
REAL SOON

The officers with their stuffed utility belts and their beeping walkie-talkies took up most of the space in the apartment. One rested a hand on Aunt Hettie and spoke to her in hushed tones. Her face reddened and paled by turns. She shook her head and replied with hissing whispers.

The other officer loomed, a dark, ominous shadow.

Mr. Killian introduced himself to the officer. "These are two of the Adams children, the eldest and the youngest. Their middle sister is at the office, answering additional questions."

Malcolm narrowed his eyes and his voice quivered. "What's going on here?"

The officer knelt before the child. "Your mother's worried about you. We're here to make sure you get home."

Casey swallowed around the growing lump in her throat. "Our mother knows where we are. We told her yesterday."

The officer looked up at her, and Casey's words died away, as did her confidence.

"She asked us to find you. She's sick with worry."

Malcolm grimaced. "Why didn't Mommy call us, then? She knows the numbers." He puffed out his chest. "Even I know the numbers. Want to hear?"

The officer ruffled Malcolm's hair. "No, thanks, Champ." Malcolm scowled and smoothed it with angry swipes.

The officer addressed Mr. Killian. "Are you transporting them?"

Mr. Killian frowned. "Just got another call in the opposite direction. Don't suppose you could see to their passage?"

The officer tipped his head toward his partner. "Depends on what the boss says."

Say something! Casey squeezed words from her strangled throat. "I have my car."

The officer's face relaxed. "Okay. Your Mom's worried something fierce, so don't dawdle."

Malcolm crossed his arms. "What about Rachel?"

Mr. Killian handed Casey a card. "She's here. Call first, though, to see if they'll allow you to take her. Okay?"

Malcolm's mouth pressed into a tight line. "Why wouldn't they let us take her?"

That's what I was thinking, kiddo.

Mr. Killian shrugged. "Just call first if you want to save yourself some trouble."

Don't like the sound of that at all.

Mr. Killian touched his hand to a non-existent hat in an old-fashioned gesture of farewell and bustled out of the apartment.

Casey gave the bulky officer a wide berth and set to re-folding the children's bedding. The fabric smoothed at her touch until small, manageable squares formed. Malcolm rescued his Teddy Bear.

"I can't believe this!" Aunt Hettie's voice punctured the whispered conversation. "What about the children?"

The officer closer to Casey blocked Aunt Hettie's worry from view. "Please calm down, Miss. Your niece can drive them home."

Although she strained to make sense of their quiet conversation, Casey could not make out the words.

Aunt Hettie shimmied around the bulky officers and knelt to embrace Casey and Malcolm. "I love you so much. You drive safe." A crooked smile forced itself across her pale face. "But you're always safe, aren't you?" She nestled into Casey's neck. "I'll see you all real soon. Okay?"

Casey whispered, "I thought the kids were staying here with you for a while."

Tears obscured Aunt Hettie's eyes. "Soon. Real soon." She pulled them to her a second more, then pushed them toward the door. "Get going now. I love you."

Casey clutched the freshly folded bedding to her chest. "Are you sure we should go?" She eyed the officers with suspicion.

The closer officer patted Malcolm's back. "Don't you worry." He escorted them over the threshold. "Do you know the way to the Protective Services Office?"

"I'll find it." She peeked around him to see Aunt Hettie's wave. "I'll see you real soon. I love you."

Real soon.

"We love you, too, Aunt Hettie."

CHAPTER TWENTY-ONE:
REST ON WINGS

The GPS on her phone guided Casey to the CYF office. Malcolm held her hand as they inquired after Rachel.

The receptionist shook her head and squinted at her computer screen. "I'm sorry, dear, but she is not here."

Panic gripped Casey. *Stay calm. Breathe.* "Where is she?"

The receptionist shifted her gaze from Malcolm's glare. "I'm sorry, but I'm not supposed to say." She leaned over the desk. "But I can tell you she's safe."

"Mr. Killian asked us to get her. Please, we just want our sister." Casey's voice trembled.

"He never should have said that without calling first."

He did say to call. She cleared her throat for another attempt. "She'll be missing us. Can we please, please take Rachel with us?"

"Does she have a cell phone?"

"No."

The receptionist frowned. "All I can tell you is she is

safe and will be at school tomorrow."

"Okay," Casey said, though nothing was. Leaden weight settled in her stomach, and her thoughts slowed. She tugged Malcolm's hand, but the little boy had something to say.

He squared his chin and took a deep breath. "You know, it isn't nice to break up families."

The receptionist blinked surprise. "We're trying to help during bad times. We don't want to break anyone apart, but we do try to protect children. That's our job."

Casey tugged at Malcolm. "Come on, honey."

He glared at the receptionist as he exited.

Once buckled in the car booster seat, he crossed his arms over his seat belt. "You should've fought harder, Casey. You always give up too easy."

His words settled like an additional brick in her stomach. *What more could I do?*

Malcolm frowned at his reflection in the car window.

What do I do now?

She started the engine and tuned into a pop radio station. *I can protect the kiddo I have with me, that's what.* She dialed Aunt Hettie, but her phone went straight to voicemail. *Maybe she's got it turned off for work.* She drove by Aunt Hettie's place. Aunt Hettie's beat up car was parked in its spot, but nobody answered the locked door. *Could the police have driven her to work? But why?*

She swung by the diner. No Aunt Hettie there.

The brick in her stomach grew to a boulder. *Can't take Malcolm home to crazy Mom. What if she's the one who called CYF, even though she's the one who hurt us? No, she wouldn't do something that bad. But it could have been the hospital staff who reported.* She blinked back tears before they could trickle out. *Gosh, my head hurts.*

Casey tried to squeeze cheerfulness into her voice. "Want to see my dorm room? We could take a nap and maybe figure this mess out."

"I don't take naps anymore, Casey. I'm a big boy."

"Oh, you don't have to nap. But I could use one."

"Is Jaimie there? And Tim?"

"They're on campus somewhere, yes."

He shrugged. "Sure."

Casey opened the window to allow the warming air to waft through the car. Something drifted in, a floating bit of brown edged with cream.

Malcolm giggled. "The butterfly likes you." He strained against the restraint and extended his finger, but the butterfly settled on Casey's shoulder like a pirate's parrot. "Its blue spots are pretty. Did you know blue's my favorite color?"

"It is, huh? Wasn't yellow your favorite, like last week?" She winked at him over the butterfly's delicate wings.

"It won't come to me." Malcolm pouted.

"I've never had a butterfly land on me before. I didn't even know they were around this early in the season." She reached across her body toward the slow-moving wings. As she brushed it with her index finger, she gasped. Profound sadness welled from within until silent tears gushed over her cheeks.

Casey pulled to the side of the road while conflicting emotions flooded her. The butterfly brought an experience of a life filled with self-doubt cut far too short, an existence unaware of its beauty and potential. Glimpses of sadness and far too little joy paled when at last the soul represented by this butterfly gave in to his depression. "Rest in peace," Casey prayed.

"Casey?" Malcolm clutched his knees. He'd taken off his belt, had his back to the door, and rocked the way Casey did when upset. "Are you okay?"

She scrubbed away the smeared makeup trails and nodded at her brother as the butterfly fluttered out the car window. "I'm sorry, honey," she sniffed. "Sometimes emotions overwhelm me."

He nodded. "Do you want me to do anything?"

"No. I'm fine now. Really. And I'm sorry."

He bit his lower lip and whispered, "I'm scared, too."

"Everything's going to be okay."

He twisted in his seat until his feet dangled above the car floor, and stared out the window. "Maybe I do want a nap."

Me, too, kid.

She drove to campus, parked and grabbed her belongings, and recited the names of the halls as she escorted Malcolm to her dorm. As she passed the aspen grove, the feeling of being watched assailed her, and she shivered.

Malcolm clung to her hand in silence.

"Here we are. This is the women's dorm building."

Malcolm yawned and rubbed his eyes.

Inside, a curly-haired blonde Casey vaguely recognized from one of her classes smiled. "Who's this cutie?"

"My kid brother wanted to see my room."

She wrinkled her nose at Malcolm, which made her look like a bunny. "Aren't you the handsomest young man?"

Malcolm's unimpressed expression bordered on rude.

The blonde laughed. "A lot of men have that reaction to me! Did you find your room okay? It is down that hall, isn't it?"

Casey's face scrunched until it bore a distrust similar to Malcolm's. "Yes."

"Great! I'm glad I didn't steer you wrong!" She waved and disappeared into her room, leaving a cloud of jasmine perfume in her wake.

When did she direct me? I wonder if she has me confused with someone else.

In the dorm room, Casey made the bed with the sheets and blanket she'd clutched during the visit at Aunt Hettie's.

Malcolm pointed to the already made bed situated along the opposite side of the room. "Who sleeps there?"

"My roommate Deirdre. Maybe you'll meet her later."

"I thought you were having sleepovers with Jaimie."

So did I, kid. "That didn't work out."

His mention of Jaimie brought sadness. Casey texted her friend. "How's everything? You busy?" No response.

Casey lifted Malcolm onto the bed and climbed up beside him. He curled into a ball and snuggled into her warmth. She brushed a lock of hair from his eyes. *What am I going to do?*

She texted Aunt Hettie and Dad. "CYF kept Rachel.

I have Malcolm."

No responses.

Malcolm snored. Casey's eyelids drooped. Before she nodded off, she texted Tim. "Thank you for being a port in the storm of my life."

CHAPTER TWENTY-TWO:
VISITING A FRIEND

A short time later, Casey woke, her little brother nestled at her side. His chest rumbled a gentle symphony of sleep, and he sucked his thumb. He hasn't done that in years.

She rolled from bed, careful not to disturb Malcolm, and checked her phone.

From Tim. "I love you, my Casey Bear. Is everything ok?"

From Dad. "I heard. I'm picking up Rachel tomorrow morning for school."

From Jaimie. "Sorry. Had 'The Doors' blasting and didn't hear you. Can't believe I never listened to them before. They're great! Amber's got all their stuff on vinyl. 'Sup witchu? Wanna come over?"

Sure would like to see Jaimie.

Casey brushed Malcolm's hair from his eyes, but he didn't stir.

Bet he'd stay asleep long enough for me to run over to Jaimie's. It's super close by.

She wrote a simple note in case he did wake, folded it to allow it to stand upright, wrote Malcolm's name on the front, and propped it on the bedside table near her brother's head. It read,

"I'll be right back. I left my phone if you want to

play a game, or you can use the paper in my bag to draw some pictures. Be very quiet and good. I love you."

She turned down the ringer on her phone and closed the door with care when she exited. With a quick dash, she reached Jaimie's room. Bass from "People are Strange" made the wood on the door vibrate beneath Casey's knock.

Jaimie flung the door wide and without a pause pulled Casey into the room. "I've missed you, girlie!" She twirled Casey onto her bed. "So much has happened. It feels like an age since we've talked. But really it hasn't been. Has it?" She spun, spreading her skirt with the breeze, until it settled like a closed flower blossom about her thin legs. "Amber'll be back soon. She's grabbing drinks from the co-op. I could text her to ask her to bring one for you."

"No, don't worry. I can't stay long."

"Oh, well, I wish you could. I miss you." She thrust her lower lip out in a pout. "Besides, I'd like you to get to know Amber. She's great. She and I share the same taste in music. She's a science major, too. And she even swims. Like me. She's thinking she might join the swim team when the season starts." Jaimie smiled. "You'll love her once you get to know her. I just know it."

I doubt it. She wasn't very nice to Deirdre. She forced a smile across taut cheeks but could not raise her gaze to meet Jaimie's. Of course, I've not told you how mean she was, or why I agreed to be Deidre's roomie.

As though on cue, Amber burst into the room. Steam escaped the small sip holes of the plastic caps, perfuming the room with heady, dark brewed coffee. "I've got your java, Mimi. Turn up the tunes, and let's get this study party started!"

Turn it up? Its pounding as loud as a nightclub in here.

Amber's sneakers screeched as she skidded to a surprised stop. "Oh, I didn't know we had a guest." She narrowed her eyes at her cardboard carry tray of coffee. "Sorry."

Casey stood and pulled her purse string tight to her chest. "It's okay. I'm leaving."

Jaimie grabbed her hand. "No! You just got here."

"I know, but I'm worried. Malcolm's asleep in my room, and I don't want him to wake and wonder where I am."

Amber smiled. "Ooh. Who's Malcolm?"

Casey shrugged. "My brother."

"Brother? In your dorm?" Amber set the coffee on her desk and clapped. "Is he a student?"

Casey nodded. "He just started school this year."

"Oh, the dear!" She twirled a strand of her hair around her finger, her manicured fingernails flashing pink. "Is he cute?"

"Well, yeah, he's cute."

Jaimie giggled, eyes glinting with mischief. "Adorable, actually, but you're too old for him. Sorry, Amber."

"Too old?" Amber pouted. "I'm only a sophomore. I can't be too old. Wait. How old is he?"

"What is he now? Seven?"

Amber moaned. "Seven? Years old? No, that's just wrong of you." She fake-slapped Casey's wrist. "Too, too young!" She grimaced at Casey. "Why'd you say he's cute if he's just a baby?"

She flipped her hair over her shoulder and retreated to her desk.

Casey furrowed her brow. Why does Amber care about my brother's age?

Jaimie stood close to Casey's side and lowered her voice. "Case, is everything okay? What's Malcolm doing on campus?"

"I have to go. I'll text later." Casey closed the door on the baffling experience.

Maybe Amber thought my brother was old enough to date. Ew.

As she rounded onto her hallway, someone darted into the alcove leading to the shower area. Something about the way she moved left Casey feeling ill-at-ease, so she hurried to her dorm.

CHAPTER TWENTY-THREE:
SECURITY GUARD

When she entered her room, Malcolm's giggles greeted her.

Shoot, he woke when I was gone.

"I'm sorry, Buddy! I tried to hurry."

Malcolm bounced from his hiding place under Casey's bed. He'd pulled the blanket from Dierdre's bed to create a fabric wall.

"Oh, no, Malcolm, that's not my blanket! It's my roommate's. We can't just help ourselves to her things."

Before Casey could retrieve the blanket, though, Diedre peeked from beneath it. "It's okay. Making the cabin was my idea, actually. I hope you don't mind."

Casey's mouth popped open with surprise. "Um, no, of course not."

"Under my bed is stuffed with bins, so we had to use yours. Hope that's okay." Deirdre shimmied out and struggled to her feet with a quiet grunt. "I used to love making hiding places when I was little."

She's smiling? What magic did you work, little brother?

Malcolm craned his neck to gaze into Dierdre's face. "You're really good at it."

Deirdre ruffled his hair. "Thanks, kid. I had lots of practice, but you're not so bad at construction yourself."

Malcolm ran a hand through his hair to put it back in place but didn't complain.

He hates having his hair messed with, yet he's smiling.

Deirdre looked out of the corner of her eye at Casey. "I assumed you'd sneak in a guy eventually, but I never imagined he'd be so..." she smiled down at Malcolm. "Sweet."

"Thanks." Malcolm imitated Deidre's alto voice. "You're not so bad yourself."

Casey stammered, "I'm sorry, Deirdre. We have a strange situation at home, and I didn't have anywhere to take him." Her voice caught in her throat. She swallowed. *I don't know if Mom's still home, if Aunt Hettie's back, if Dad's able to get Rachel.* Tears prickled, and Casey realized she rocked on the balls of her feet. *I don't know what to do.*

"Hey," Deirdre placed a gentle hand on Casey's upper arm, her brows raised high toward her hairline. "Not a worry. I don't mind." She blinked away her eye contact and turned a smile on Malcolm. "He can be our good luck charm. Right, kid?"

Malcolm made an exaggerated nod. "Yep." He pointed to his chest. "And since I'm a superhero, I'll keep you girls safe."

Deirdre concealed a smile behind a nose-scratch. "Well, isn't that convenient? We'll have our own security guard."

Casey's heart slowed to a more normal pace. She whispered, "You don't mind?"

Deirdre shook her head. "Nah." She pulled a footlocker from beneath her bed, opened it, and removed granola bars. She extended them. "Want one?"

The wave of relief left Casey weak in her knees. "Thank you so much, Deirdre. He won't be here long."

"It's okay. As long as he's quiet, I can't imagine anyone reporting us." She handed Malcolm a bar and peeled back the wrapper on hers. "Say, kid, you don't snore, do you?"

"Snore? No, I don't think so." He took a bite of his granola. Crumbles slipped from his mouth. "Do I, Casey?"

"No, you don't snore." *She's not demanding an explanation, not threatening to have me expelled.* Casey swayed in preparation of a self-stimulating bout of rocking but caught herself. "Deirdre, thank you. I'm so grateful."

Deirdre shrugged and sat at her desk. "Got to get my essay written now." She winked at Malcolm. "You can stay in the cabin if you want."

"Thanks." Malcolm wriggled under the bed. In a none-too-quiet whisper, he said, "I like your roommate, Casey. She's really cool."

Casey studied the back of Deirdre's head. "Yeah, she sure is."

Deirdre turned in her chair and smiled at them. "You two aren't so bad yourselves."

CHAPTER TWENTY-FOUR:
MESSAGE IN THE NIGHT

Casey woke with her feet hanging from the bed, Malcolm's elbow in her face. He reposed spread-eagle. A beatific smile stretched across his cherub face. His chest rose and fell with the abandon of security. Deirdre faced the wall, but from the regularity of her breathing, she slept as well.

Something tapped at the window, a soft scrape too insistent to be a tree branch. Casey eased from the bed, pushed back the cotton window panel, and peeked through the blinds. She jumped back with a gasp, heart racing. Casey pressed her palm over her mouth to suppress a giggle. *It's an owl.* A ghostly snowy owl larger than her forearm rubbed its beak back and forth against the outside window frame. *I've never seen an owl this close. What on earth is it doing?*

Moonlight flooded the back courtyard around the women's dormitory, casting everything into stark contrasts of silver and shadow. Someone pushed a rickety wire cart along the uneven pathways, keeping to the darkness. Not much could be discerned of the person's features since layers of clothing obscured, but from the cautious walk, the hunch of shoulders, and the scarf-wrapped, bowed head, the best guess was an older woman, probably homeless, prowled for scraps and cast-offs.

Casey's breath fogged the window, creating crystalline patterns as it cooled. Casey swiped the wintery obstruction of her view.

The owl shifted on its narrow perch, feathers ruffled, alert. It turned huge, unblinking eyes to Casey.

She whispered, "Do you have an invitation to a wizarding school for me, or have you come for the lady down there?"

The owl's "hoot" sent a thrill through Casey. Her mouth went dry, and her hands shook as she searched the ground beneath her window.

The homeless woman shuffled, gentle scritch-scritches of inadequate footwear against stone. Her cart groaned gentle complaints of rusted years of misuse. Casey's vision blurred, but not from condensation on the windowpanes. Her breath gasped, and she clapped a hand over her mouth to stifle a moan. With a quick glimpse at the sleepers in the room, she grabbed her jacket, shoved her feet into shoes without benefit of socks, and allowed the door to close behind her retreat with a soft click.

She rushed to the back of the building where she knew she'd find the woman in the throes of death. Gasps tumbled over sobs as a low moan ripped through Casey. Her hair flew behind her as she ran to the woman and fell to her knees at her side.

The owl perched on a bush disguising a rubbish can near the maintenance entrance, its head bowed as though in prayer.

Casey sobbed as she cradled the woman's head.

The woman's breath reeked of decayed teeth and sour breath, but she smiled up at Casey. Her voice sounded like gravel settling before a rockslide. "You're a good 'un." She patted Casey's wrist with a hand encased in several pairs of cheap stretch gloves. "I'll be going now."

The owl swept over her with the muffled wings of a night predator, and the old homeless lady gasped in Casey's lap, an ominous rattle that ended with an oppressive silence.

The owl disappeared into the night, silent as a spirit, mysterious and beautiful.

Casey removed her coat and bunched it under the lady's head and whispered, "Safe passage."

I never even know their names. Well, not usually. I cry for them, but I don't know anything about them except they're dying.

Casey wiped the slick of tears from her cheeks. The woman stretched on the ground at her feet stared unblinking at the star-filled sky.

I guess since they don't know me, either, it's better that way.

Casey stood and wiped debris from her knees before she walked to the corner of the building where the blue light of the campus emergency call box glowed. She shivered as she pushed the pulsing orange call button. "Please send help. I found a woman dead behind the women's dorm."

Deep, circular breathing, eyes closed, calmed her before the police arrived. After answering their questions, Casey reclaimed her jacket from under the woman's head. It smelled slightly of tuna fish and bore soil from its task. *I'll have to wash it.*

With a sigh, she returned to her room. She slipped out of her shoes and climbed into her bed as best she could around the splayed form of her little brother. *Sure do take up a lot of space, little man.* She kissed his forehead before she drifted off to sleep again.

CHAPTER TWENTY-FIVE:
MOURNING CLOAKS CAUGHT IN AMBER

A different bird sang at the window when morning stained the panes. A robin puffed out its russet chest and sang with gusto.

Casey groaned. Her back ached from odd sleep positions, and her head swam from lack of sleep. Deidre turned away to hide a chuckle while Malcolm luxuriated in an exaggerated yawn and stretch. His tousled hair stood on end, and his shirt rose up to reveal his belly button. "What's for breakfast?" He eyed the footlocker under Deidre's bed from whence the granola appeared yesterday. "I'm starving."

Casey grabbed her comb from her purse and straightened Malcolm's hair as he dodged her attempts.

"Hold still. I've got to get you to school, and you don't want to be late."

He swatted at the comb. Casey connected with a smoothing stroke of the instrument.

"My hair's fine. Pwease!"

"Hurry and wash up. I may not have a change of clothes for you, but that doesn't mean you get to stink."

He scooped up Casey's fallen jacket and threw it at her with a cock-eyed grin. "You're the stinky one."

The scent of the owl's woman from last night lingered within its fibers. Casey buried her face in its folds and inhaled as though she could discern the life from the trace that remained, a bloodhound in search of the departed soul. With care, she set it on her bed as though tucking it in for a nap.

Malcolm stumbled from their small restroom and frowned. "Will we see Rachel at school?"

"I sure hope so." Casey ran the comb through her snarls, slipped on a clean outfit, and waved goodbye to Deirdre. "I hope you have a good day."

"You, too, Casey. Malcolm, I hope I see you again soon."

As Casey tried to herd Malcolm through the door, he feinted left, then dodged beneath her backpack to rush to Deirdre. He stopped just short of a hug, but he blinked up at her with sincerity. "I hope to see you again, too." With a quick jerk of his chin, he returned to Casey and headed for her car.

"I like Deirdre. She's nice." He said as they stepped into relatively balmy weather. Unpaved ground squelched beneath their passage. Malcolm grabbed her hand and swung it as they walked.

The breezes raised gooseflesh along Casey's bare arms, but for a change, she didn't mind the sensation. "I like her, too."

Outside of the Quad, Malcolm squealed. "Ooh, Casey, it's the butterfly from yesterday!"

Indeed, a butterfly alighted on Casey's shoulder. Black outlined its shiny mahogany wings, while from its bottom sprouted cream frills edged with cobalt spots. A second butterfly joined the first, and then a third.

Malcolm gasped. "Where are they all coming from?"

Casey whispered lest she frighten them from their perch on her shoulder. "Not sure."

As they stood and admired the butterflies, a woman approached. "Hey, Casey! I guess this is your little brother." Her gaze puffed over Malcolm, but her mouth dropped open when she saw Casey's shoulder. "Oh my goodness! Mourning Cloaks." She circled close enough for her to sigh minty breath into Casey's face. "These are the first butterflies of the season."

Casey's heart plunged. "And they're called," she swallowed hard, "Mourning Cloaks?"

"Uh huh." Amber leaned close. "I'm something of a lepidopterist, actually. Goes along with my studies."

"Oh?" Casey tried to force the tremble from her voice. "What's your major?"

"Entomology. I thought you knew." Her voice took on a far-away sound. "I'll earn my Bachelor of Science in Biology and Natural Sciences and specialize in studying bugs in grad school."

Malcolm's mouth fell open. "You can study bugs at college?"

Amber rolled her head toward him as though moving through molasses. Her words drolled with the same sarcastic slowness. "Of course. Don't you know anything?"

Malcolm scoffed, his cheeks reddened. "I know lots of things, but I'm not in college, so I didn't know that. I thought it was cool. But if you're studying it, maybe not."

Amber narrowed her eyes, then threw back her head and laughed.

The sound startled the butterflies who flittered together into a rare, cloudless sky.

Amber's gaze followed their progress.

"We'll be going. Take care." Casey rested a guiding hand on Malcolm's shoulder and ushered him along the path to her car.

In a low, growling voice, Malcolm said, "I don't like her."

Casey glanced over her shoulder to Amber who followed the butterflies. *I may agree with you. Not sure yet.*

At the elementary school, an unfamiliar crossing guard waved them to a parking spot. *They've had a hard time replacing the other lady, the one I saw die.* Casey shivered.

"Look, there's Rachel!" Malcolm all but bounced out of the car in his haste to see his sister.

Rachel waved from outside the front door, a wide smile across her delicate features.

"Wait for me, Malcolm, and give me your hand, please." Casey hurried to escort him, happy to rush to her sister. Tears streaked all of their faces as they hugged their greetings.

"Are you all right? Where did they take you? You need a cell phone! Gosh, I missed you! I was so worried, I thought I'd be sick." Questions and statements tumbled over one another, eager as affection-seeking puppies, when the initial bell advised students to get to classes.

"You go on inside, Malcolm," Rachel said. "I'll see you at the end of the day, okay?"

Malcolm pressed his lips together in imitation of his narrowed eyes. "Why aren't you coming?"

"I am, but I have to tell Casey something first."

Malcolm crossed his arms. "Oh no you don't. No secrets. You can tell me, too. I'm a big boy."

Rachel crossed her arms, a mirror to Malcolm. "Anyone who has to say 'I'm a big boy' isn't. Now move along." She shooed him.

"Fine, but Casey'll tell me later, so there." He stuck out his tongue, turned with a huff, and stormed into the building.

Once he left, Rachel wheeled on her sister. "Did you tell those people the truth about what happened? Why we went to the hospital?"

Casey dropped her gaze to the sidewalk. She spoke slow and quiet to the asphalt cracks. "I told them I was clumsy and fell. I said I didn't know what happened to you."

Rachel stomped her foot into Casey's field of vision. "Darn it!" Her face contorted with reddened annoyance. She lowered her voice. "Look at me, Casey. Here." She tapped her cheek until Casey looked her in the eye. "You have to tell them what happened. Now. Today." She punctuated each word with a pause. "You have to."

"But Momma..."

Rachel hissed her words. "Momma blamed Aunt Hettie. Said she saw Aunt Hettie do it. They arrested her. Aunt Hettie's in jail because Momma lied to protect herself."

The world around Casey spun. *Arrested?* Hushed words expelled in a surprised gush. "Oh my gosh."

Rachel nodded, eyebrows raised. She placed a hand

on Casey's arm. "You see what I mean. You have to go now and tell them."

Casey felt queasy. "I will. I'll go now."

Rachel hugged her. "Just tell the truth."

Casey nodded and repeated, "I will. I'll go now."

Those words became her mantra as she walked weak-kneed to the car and drove to the CYF office. "I need to talk to Mr. Killian. I think that's his name. I have to tell him what happened."

The receptionist pushed back her chair and escorted Casey to a room with a flickering fluorescent light. "I'll get him."

Casey paced as she recited the events to the social worker.

"Why didn't you tell me this yesterday?"

Casey rocked, sick to her stomach, head an angry symphony of throbs. "I didn't want anyone to be in trouble."

"Not telling the truth the first time has caused all kinds of trouble, actually." He stomped from the room, the door waving with his departure.

Casey blinked at the door, numb with reaction. She whispered to the room. "I told the truth, so I'll go now." She pulled her purse strap over her shoulder and hugged the bag itself to her chest. In the car, she slumped over the steering wheel and typed a text message to Aunt Hettie. "We told the truth, so please come home now." *I know the police are the ones who decide if she can come home, but I want her to know we miss her.*

A message came through, but not from Aunt Hettie. It registered from Jaimie. "Meet me for coffee, please?"

She didn't lift her head. With the phone in her lap,

she typed her reply. "I'll be there in about a half hour. Is that okay?"

When she lifted her head, a butterfly had alighted on her windshield. With slow determination, the Mourning Cloak opened and closed its wings. Closed, it appeared dull as a dried leaf. Open, it shimmered like satin. Casey opened her window, and it flitted with an apple blossom scented breeze into the car.

"So you are here for me?" She asked it. Its feet tickled when it landed on the back of her hand, and although it weighed nearly nothing, Casey felt the now familiar burden of sadness, regret, fear, joys, and hope. Silent tears gave way to a torrent of despair for a soul she'd never met in life.

When the emotion borne by the butterfly released its hold on her, Casey cried for her mother, lost in her own madness, for her family, caught up in it with her. She prayed for the soul she imagined transported by this delicate creature - or was the butterfly a representation of a soul?

Casey tried to force her thoughts through the books of folk beliefs and superstitions about death she'd read in the autumn. Emotion flooded her memories, though, and left her with only the sensation of a small insect floating out the window to continue its journey.

She brushed her sleeve across her face and called after the butterfly, "I don't know if I help at all, but I pray it's a successful journey, butterfly."

When it flew from view, Casey remembered a section from Dr. Krochalis' Comparative Religions class last semester on death beliefs, but from what she recalled, the varied cultures could only agree on one thing. Winged things often conveyed spirits to their afterlife.

She wound up the window and drove to campus, parked, and walked to the coffee shop. The breezes perturbed the hairs on her arms until they stood at attention.

She texted Aunt Hettie as she walked. "Rachel and I told the officers what happened. I hope you're home now. I'm so sorry. I didn't know Mom blamed you."

She entered the coffee shop, warm with brews and stuffed with students, and found Jaimie whose smile, embrace, and waiting coffee welcomed Casey. She patted the raised stool beside her and said, "How's it going, girlfriend?"

Casey scaled the chair, leaned on the elevated round table, and shrugged. "It's been a bit of a mess, actually."

Jaimie rested an uncustomarily still hand on Casey's. "I've been worried."

Before Casey said anything further, Amber took the third seat opposite them. "Hey, ladies! I thought I'd find you here! What a day, huh? And it looks like it wants to rain soon. Stupid weather! Hey, Casey, you'll never guess what I found. Look."

She pushed a coffee cup across the table.

Casey wrinkled her brow, annoyed with the intrusion, confused by the cup.

"Well, open it!" She inclined her head toward the baristas and took a sip from a second coffee cup. "They even gave me a napkin soaked in disinfectant, so I'll be ready to pin and stretch it in about a week or two."

Casey's hands shook with dread as she opened the plastic lid. Inside the thick paper cup, a Mourning

Cloak butterfly rested atop a pungent, pine-scented napkin, unmoving. Dead.

Casey screamed and pushed the cup away. She covered her mouth and stared at Amber. "Why'd you do that? Kill it?" She blinked through tears at Amber. "I don't understand."

Shock played on Amber's features, but a slight smile tugged the left corner of her mouth upward. She shrugged. "I told you I loved butterflies. I thought you shared my enthusiasm."

Casey jumped from the stool, bile in her throat. Without another word, she fled the coffee shop, left Jaimie and her unfinished latte and the poor butterfly trapped and killed by Amber.

CHAPTER 26:
FACE IN THE WINDOW

Maybe some butterflies convey souls, or maybe some souls become butterflies, but maybe some are just insects who evolve from caterpillars. Casey sniffed back angry reproaches. *Why'd Amber kill it if she likes butterflies?*

Her meandered path took her not to her next class but instead to Dr. Krochalis' closed office door. Casey knocked despite the sign hung outside announcing the visit fell outside of office hours. *Please be in.* No answer. Casey sighed. *Darn it.*

She glanced at her phone. Nothing from Aunt Hettie, but a text from Tim. "I love you, beautiful! Meet me for dinner?"

She typed back, "Sure. If I can."

If she hurried, she could still slip into class.

She rushed across campus beneath a sky ominous with heavy clouds. *Guess Amber's right. It looks like rain.* Her gaze slid from the cloud cover to the women's dorm. A face stared from a window, a face remarkably like her own. *Is that my window?* She noted the location of the scrawny tree outside the maintenance entrance. *I think so.* When she sought the face at the window, it was gone.

Radio static and muffled communication drew her reluctant attention. A campus police officer conversed with two uniformed officers who bore a striking resemblance to the men who arrested Aunt Hettie. *Are they here for me?*

Something in their conversation sparked her attention. The campus cop pointed to the women's dorm. "She's up there. I just talked with her." He shrugged. "Why I called, right? When I was sure I knew where to find her." He gave directions.

Casey stiffened when she heard. *That's my room number!*

Ignoring her palpitating heart and headache and fighting every urge to run and hide, Casey approached the authority figures. "Hello, I'm Casey Adams. Are you looking for me?"

The campus officer knitted his brows. "Hey, I told you to stay in your dorm."

Casey tipped her head, confused. Her gaze slid and danced. "I didn't talk with you, sir. I'm sorry."

The campus office protested, "What about me telling you to stay put didn't you understand?"

"I've never talked to you. Sorry."

The trooper interrupted the campus officer's further protestations, gaze intent on Casey. "But you're Casey Adams?"

Casey noticed the scuffs on the trooper's otherwise shining black leather shoes. "Yes, sir."

The officers nodded at one another. One removed a notebook and pen. "We have to talk to you about your report at the CYF office, Ms. Adams."

Casey followed them to a bench beneath a budding elm tree. The campus cop walked away with a shake of his head and a huffed breath. She studied the patterns made by the shed petals of a nearby crabapple as she rehashed her statement. She followed an insect as it floated a meandering path among emerging blooms. She spoke when spoken to and fell silent while they recorded her responses. Anything to distract from the awful truth of dysfunctional home life.

The older of the officers stood. "One last question, Miss. Are you the same Casey Adams who reported the death of the vagrant woman last night?"

Casey's gaze shifted to the spot where the woman had fallen. Her lip trembled, and she nodded.

His voice softened. "You've had quite a couple of days, haven't you?"

Casey's chin dropped to her collar, and she swayed with the rhythm of the spring breeze.

He cleared his throat. "Well, take care. We'll be in touch if we have any other questions."

Casey allowed the air to caress her long after the officers left.

CHAPTER TWENTY-SEVEN:
A BREAK-IN AND A BREAK-THROUGH

"Casey?" Deirdre edged close as though worried she might frighten Casey. "Are you okay?"

Casey blinked into the afternoon sunlight at her roommate. "Yeah, I'm okay."

Deirdre sunk to a crouch, putting her on Casey's eye level. "Are you sure? You look a bit - agitated."

Casey considered herself. *Oh my gosh, how long have I been rocking on this bench?* The sun nestled above the tallest trees, sliding closer to setting. "Shoot, my classes!"

Deirdre raised her hands to placate. "I think they're done for today. You don't have night classes, do you?"

Casey shook her head. *What do I have on my schedule?* The days swum in her imagination, a swirl meaningless of dates and words.

"Do you need me to call someone for you?" Dierdre's dark eyes abandoned their usual hooded appearance, widened with concern. Or was it fear?

Call? Who could I call? What do I have to say? She retrieved her cell phone and noticed pending messages. *Wonder who wrote to me? Rachel needs a cell phone.*

Rachel! Malcolm! They should be home from school. Is Mom at home? Will she hurt them?

Casey bolted to her feet, dizzy with worry. "I have to go home."

Deirdre had fallen to her bottom when Casey leapt to her feet. She scrambled to her feet and brushed leaves and dirt from her butt with one hand, yet she kept the other extended toward Casey, palm exposed. "Woah there. I don't think you should drive."

"What? I'm fine." *Aren't I? I do feel a bit spacey. Detached.*

"Casey, please don't get behind the wheel of a car. I don't think it would be a good idea." The hoods slid over Deirdre's eyes which deepened their shadowy appearance and darkened the sleepless circles.

Thoughts of self-harm flooded Casey. Not her own thoughts. Deirdre's. *Poor girl. What happened to her? Can't worry about that now, though.* "I have to go home."

"Okay." Deirdre swallowed hard. "I'll come with you. Give me like four seconds to throw these into the room, okay?"

"You don't have to come." *I don't know what I'm going to find.*

"I'm coming. And you should get a jacket. You're absolutely covered with gooseflesh."

I am. Wasn't I wearing a jacket earlier?

The two entered their dorm building, Deirdre casting furtive glances, Casey lost in her thoughts. They ignored the boisterous knot of women at the entrance of their hall and continued to their room. They froze in place and stared. Their door gaped, open to anyone.

Deirdre's voice trembled. "You have to keep the door closed and locked when we're not in there."

Clarity infiltrated Casey's foggy thoughts. "But you left after I did this morning. I didn't come back after I took Malcolm to school."

Cautious, they entered. Their closet doors also hung on the hinges, open. Their drawers lay upside down outside their dressers. Papers littered their desks.

Deirdre covered her mouth with her hand.

A voice behind them made them jump. "It was a panty raid, we think." A woman with bushy hair leaned into their room through the still-open doorway. "Take inventory. We're getting a complaint together, and we'll be checking to see if the security cameras caught anything."

Deirdre bit into her lip. "So it wasn't just our room?"

The woman shook her head. "Nah, looks like they got almost everyone on this floor."

Deirdre picked up papers from the floor and stacked them in piles while Casey put things to rights. She stuffed wadded paper into the wastebasket after setting it upright, refolded the towels and washcloths, and rewound the toilet paper. At the mirror above the sink, she froze. Written in red lipstick was, "I see you."

Deirdre slammed her hand on her desk, startling Casey. "Who would do this?" Her face contorted, however, as she knelt before her capsized pink tote. Her hands worked with frantic speed as she restored order and inventoried. "No." Her search grew frantic. "My medicine," she whispered. "It's gone!"

Casey waved to the Resident Advisor. "Whoever did this stole something from Deirdre. And they left a message." She pointed to the mirror.

The R.A. rubbed her temple. "What the hell's that supposed to mean? 'I see you.'" She ran her hands through her hair until it grew as agitated as her tone. Of Deirdre she asked, "Are you sure your medicine's missing? Nobody else is reporting stolen goods. Not even panties, which rules out a frat prank."

Deirdre's voice verged on hysterics. "I always keep them in this bin. They're not here now."

"Fine. I'll get a form. We'll call the cops and make a report. What kind of medicine do you take?"

Deirdre fell silent. Color rose through her cheeks. "Um, don't worry about it. They were for sleep. I had something to help me sleep."

The RA eyed her with suspicion. "And you don't want to report their theft now?"

Deirdre stared into the bin and shook her head.

"Alrighty then. I'll be on my way." The RA left the door open to the chaos in the hallway.

Casey could not find her jacket, so she pulled a hoodie over her head. "I'm sorry about your, um, medicine."

Deirdre continued to stare where the pill bottles should be. "They were old, really, but having them made me feel better. I mean, there are lots of ways to... Never mind."

"Lots of ways to commit suicide?" *Shoot, that was unfiltered. She looks shocked.*

"Wha-what do you mean?"

Casey shifted her weight and studied the floorboards. "When I can't sleep, my Aunt Mae used to warm milk. She moved away a few years back, though, and she died." Casey pictured Aunt Mae's kind face. "So when my kid sister or brother can't sleep, I make them warm milk. Or chamomile tea." She moved her toe along the laminate. "Aunt Hettie likes tea."

Deirdre dropped onto her bed, white faced and open mouthed. She whispered, "Why would you say that? About suicide?"

Casey's head throbbed. "Sometimes I say things without thinking. I'm sorry."

Deirdre's stare remained unflinching. "I've thought about it. Suicide." Her nostrils flared. "I'm not proud of it. I've not tried it. But I've thought about it."

Casey shook her head, numb.

Deirdre narrowed her eyes. "You knew. Didn't you?"

Casey shrugged.

She raised her chin, defiant. "I've never told anyone."

"Maybe you should. You know. Tell someone. Talk about it. A psychologist or something. Do you know Dr. Bridges?"

Deirdre shook her head. "No. I don't know Dr. Bridges. And I don't talk about it." She glared. "And I don't want anyone else talking about it for me."

Casey nodded. "It's a personal matter."

Deirdre leaned in, aggressive and keen. "Then why'd you bring it up? How'd you know?"

Casey's world swayed, back and forth. "Some people wear intentions like clothing around themselves."

Deirdre frowned. "You see things?"

Casey's skin boiled. "Sometimes. I don't mean to. I'm sorry."

They remained silent, Deirdre fixed in a stare, Casey in an agonized oscillation both figurative and literal.

Deirdre slapped her hands on the mattress and rose to her feet. "Stop. You're making me dizzy. No wonder you're so skinny. Do you ever hold still?"

Casey steadied herself. "I'm sorry."

"You apologize too much. You know that?"

"I do? I'm -"

"Sorry. Yeah. I get it. Listen, we'll try that chamomile tea sometime. I don't like milk, though. But do me a favor, huh? Keep your visions to yourself. It's kinda freaky."

"I know. I'm -"

"Sorry. Let's go. I'll clean the rest of this after we check on your family." A half smile played at the corner of her lips. "See, you're not the only observant one. Besides, I miss our bodyguard."

"You don't have to come."

"I know, but do you think I want to stay here," she swept the room with an open hand, "alone? No, thank you. Besides," she snagged her coat and an umbrella, "you're in no fit state to drive."

CHAPTER TWENTY-EIGHT:
SIZING UP

I can't take her to my home. How do I get out of this?

Deirdre tapped her foot and motioned at the door. "Coming?"

"Why are you so keen to come?"

Deirdre sighed and closed the door. "Told you. I don't like the idea of being here alone at the moment. And I don't have to be psychic to see you're dealing with some serious shit. Nobody should have to go through that sort of stuff on their own."

"I'm not going through it on my own. I've got my Dad and-" she gulped back tears, "Aunt Hettie. And Tim. And-" another gulp and a whispered, "Jaimie."

Deirdre chewed her lip as she studied Casey. "So call them. Your family and friends and see if they'll drive with you. I mean, I could go to the Quad or the library or something until you get back. Don't worry about me."

"It's not that I don't appreciate you..."

Deirdre crossed her arms over her chest and pressed her lips together. "Yeah, and you're sorry if you've hurt my feelings."

Casey's head snapped up to search Deirdre's face. *Shoot, never thought about that. Did I hurt her feelings?*

"Don't worry. I won't off myself while you're gone." She pulled her jacket off and tossed it onto her bed. "Sheesh, and people call me odd."

"Why would anyone call you odd?"

An amused grimace crossed Deirdre's face. "You mean that. Don't you?" She chuckled and shook her head. "I am odd." She rolled her eyes. "I know it, and I own it." She shrugged. "It's ok." She flopped onto her bed, palms slapping the mattress.

Casey took out her phone and texted Tim. "Could you come to my house with me?" She glanced at her roommate. "And maybe Deirdre?"

Tim's immediate response. "Sure. But Deirdre? Your roomie?"

"Yes."

"Why's she coming?"

Instead of answering, Casey wrote, "See you in ten?"

"K."

Casey slid her phone into her pocket. "You really want to meet more of my crazy family?"

Deirdre raised her eyebrows. "I didn't think you wanted me to come."

Casey noticed the scuffs on her shoes. "Figure if you get to know me, you won't consider yourself odd at all."

Deirdre smiled. "Thanks."

Casey twirled a strand of hair around her finger and tugged. "We're meeting Tim at the car. You'll like him. He's a good guy."

"Can't wait." She slipped her arms through her

jacket.

"Say, you don't see my coat, do you? The red one. I know I had it earlier. But I don't see it now."

They looked together, but neither found it.

Casey shrugged. "Oh well. I guess it'll turn up. My hoodie'll have to do."

They locked the dorm door on their way out.

Tim waited on the path to the car. He hesitated in midstep, a smile on his face, until Casey returned his gaze and nodded. He wrapped his arms around her, and she melted into his hug.

Although they stepped apart, Tim kept his hand between Casey's shoulders. He extended his other hand. "You must be Deirdre. I'm Tim. Nice to meet you."

With a hooded expression, she shook his hand and inclined her head.

As they walked to the parking area, birds chirped. Tim swung Casey's hand as they walked and stole dreamy looks at her. "What's the game plan, Boss?"

Deirdre thrust her hands deep into her pockets. "She wants to go home to check on her family, but I didn't want her driving on her own."

Tim blinked, quiet for several paces. "How's your concussion, Casey?"

Deirdre glanced through a tuft of coarse-clipped bangs at Casey. "Concussion?"

Casey thought of the dull pain chasing through her head and muddying her thoughts. She shrugged. "Achy."

Deirdre thudded alongside, trampling the young grass. "So big guy, did your dorm get broken into?"

Tim's steps faltered. "No. Why?"

"Ours did. Our whole floor, apparently, was struck."

Tim's face paled. "Was anyone hurt?"

Deirdre grimaced. "No, you ghoul."

"Deirdre, that's not nice." Casey squeezed Tim's hand. "They took some stuff and made a mess."

Deirdre frowned. "Used my lipstick to write a message on our mirror, too."

Tim stopped and pulled Casey close. "A message? What did it say?"

Deirdre turned and crossed her arms. "Something like 'I see you,' right Casey?"

Casey nodded. "The RA's on it. I have to get home, though. Please, I have to get home." She felt every second as though it pounded upon her.

They reached the cars. Tim lifted Casey's chin and whispered, "Are you okay?"

Casey nodded without making eye contact.

He studied her face, worry etched into lines upon his brow. "Want me to drive?"

Casey shrugged. "Sure. But let's go, please."

He opened her car's passenger side door for her. "My lady."

Casey slipped inside.

He opened the back door for Deirdre and raised his eyebrows.

Deirdre glared, but slumped into the back seat.

Billie Holiday's gritty voice serenaded them when the engine roared to life. Tim looked into the rearview at Deirdre.

"What's your musical poison, Deirdre?"

"What do you mean?"

"What do you like to listen to?"

Deirdre stared out the window. "Anything, I guess."

Casey turned in her seat and smiled. "Tim used to be in a band called 'Stages of Grief.'"

Deirdre smirked. "Of course he was."

Tim pulled from campus. "So, what's your major, Deirdre?"

"Electrical Engineering. Why?"

Tim chuckled. "Just making conversation. You know, first meeting and all."

"Sizing up the girlfriend's roommate, eh?"

Tim patted Casey's leg when she bristled. "I suppose so. Just like you're probably sizing up the roommate's boyfriend." He grinned into the rearview. "How'm I doing so far?"

Deirdre glared out her window. "Not sure."

CHAPTER TWENTY-NINE:
SMILE BACK

The two had discussed classes, hobbies, wishes, and music by the time they reached Casey's home. Casey watched the scenery blur into pearly streaks as they moved on to favorite pets. Tim loved dogs, while Deirdre preferred the independence of cats. When the subject of family came up, however, Deirdre turned away, arms crossed, and grew snarky. "Bet you come from a perfect family, don't you, Boy Scout?"

Tim shrugged. "No family's perfect, but I'm pretty blessed in the family department. My parents love my brother and me. And each other. We have a decent house and enough food. Yeah, they're pretty great, and yeah, I know how unusual that is these days." He squeezed Casey's hand. He glanced into the rearview mirror. "Good guess on the Boy Scout, by the way. I earned my Eagle in my senior year of high school. Didn't think I'd get it done before I aged out, but somehow, I did."

Casey furrowed her brow. "Eagle? What's that?"

"It's the highest award in Boy Scouting. For my project, I cleaned up the cemetery." He jerked his head toward the place as they drove by. "Identified some of the misplaced tombstones where kids had moved them to play football and stuff. Washed graffiti and years of wear from them. Restored the iron fencing."

Casey blinked out the window at the place. The Black Dog who greeted her before stepped from behind a crypt, tail a-whirl. *Bet nobody but me sees you, Dog.* Apple blossom petals pale as ghosts drifted on gentle breezes like a dreamy scene from a Ridley Scott movie.

Deirdre sounded interested despite herself. "What inspired that project?"

Tim's shoulder muscles bunched beneath his jacket when he shrugged. "Not sure. Respect for the departed, maybe? I played football there when I was too young to realize how disrespectful it was." He chewed the corner of his lip. "Weird, though, isn't it, Case? Like a premonition or something."

Casey blinked as though telegraphing confusion. "Premonition?"

Tim shook his head. "Not sure what I mean, but we two have become much more acquainted with death than I'd have believed when I wore a younger man's clothes."

Casey dropped her gaze to study her hands, unable to keep her thoughts steady.

Deirdre thumped her head against the window with a snort. "Who needs death as an acquaintance?"

A Marcus Aurelius quote from Classics class came unbidden to Casey. "Death smiles at us all; all we can do is smile back."

Once parked in the driveway, Casey turned to the two of them. "Maybe you should stay here. I don't know what to expect."

Tim kissed the back of her hand. "I'm here to help you, Casey. I'll do whatever you wish."

Deirdre humphed. "Yeah, well, that's all well and good, but I'm not staying cooped up in this car with Mr. White Hat any longer." She stepped from the car and opened Casey's door. "Besides, there's nothing you can show me that I haven't already seen."

Casey looked into her roommate's care-worn face and believed her. "Ok, let's go."

Casey hesitated at the broken back screen door. *Should I knock?* As she hesitated, the inner door swung open. Malcolm grinned at her. "Sister! I missed you!" He pushed through the screen door and rushed to wrap chubby arms around Deirdre's legs. "And you brought my friend!"

Tim laughed. "Hey, little buddy! Good to see you! I heard you visited the campus. Wish I'd have known. I could've stopped by."

Malcolm stiffened. "We had fun without you."

Casey pushed her eyebrows toward her hairline. "Malcolm!"

Malcolm glared at Tim a second, then his head drooped. "Sorry."

Tim chuckled. "It's okay."

"Is Rachel home? Where's Daddy?" Casey hesitated at the threshold.

"Rachel's in her room, and Daddy's talking to Aunt Hettie."

"Aunt Hettie! Is she here?"

Malcolm nodded, eyes wide. "Uh huh."

Casey made to run into the house, but something in her brother's mannerisms stopped her. "Malcolm, where's Mom?"

Malcolm scuffed the dirt at his feet. "Nobody knows where Mom went."

Chills raced up Casey's spine. "Nobody knows?"

"Uh-uh. When police came to talk to her, Mom had gone."

"Gone where?"

Malcolm stomped. "Casey, I told you, nobody knows."

Casey scanned the yard as though expecting to see her mother hiding among the rhododendron leaves. Although burgeoning with new life, the familiar contours concealed no ill-intentioned parent. No black dog lurked nearby, either, and no look-alike shape-shifter leered from behind the emerging herb garden Casey'd planted with her aunts before Malcolm was born. She forced herself to look into the empty upstairs windows and shuddered.

As though sensing her apprehension, Malcolm, Deirdre, and Tim stepped closer to Casey. Tim slipped an arm around her waist and Malcolm claimed her opposite hand. Deirdre glanced around, nostrils flared. She patted Casey's arm above Malcolm's messy-haired head. "Lead the way. We're with you, Casey."

Casey forced a smile and stepped inside.

CHAPTER THIRTY:
BAD PENNY

"Casey! Tim!" Rachel burst from the back stairwell and executed a flying embrace that encompassed both Casey and Tim. Tears streaked her face. "Oh my gosh, it's good to see you! Did you hear? They arrested Aunt Hettie! Aunt Hettie! As if she'd ever hurt anyone! But she's out now. Just got here."

Malcolm nodded. "A police car brought her. I got to turn the red and blue lights on."

Rachel smiled. "Yeah, that officer was cute." With a sudden intake of breath, widened eyes, and a delicate hand to her reddened throat, Rachel amended, "for an older guy, you know." She stole a glance at Tim who smiled at her.

Rachel stepped back, eyes wild with incredulity. "Wait," she tilted her head toward Deirdre. "That's not Jaimie."

Casey rested her trembling hand on Rachel's bruised cheek, a sort of test to assure her solid reality.

Rachel flinched away with a frown.

Tim interceded. "Rachel, this is Deirdre, Casey's roommate."

Rachel's eyes clouded with skepticism as she appraised Deirdre.

Malcolm craned his neck to look from Rachel to Deirdre. "This is our sister, Rachel. She got stolen. But now she's back." He tugged Rachel to whisper in her ear. "El, didn't I tell you she looks like Wonder Woman?"

The smile that pulled at Rachel's lips found a mirror on Deirdre's mouth. "Oh, so this is the girl you went on and on about," Rachel whispered to Malcolm in response. "Well, she's tall enough to be an Amazon, I guess."

Casey craned to peer into the living room. "Is that where Daddy and Aunt Hettie are? Do you think I should go see them?"

Rachel pushed her toward the arched doorway. "Yeah. They'll want to see you."

As Casey stepped toward the living room, Rachel whispered, "You'd think I was the oldest, the way I have to look out for Casey all the time." A stolen glance over her shoulder revealed Rachel twirling her hair and smiling up at Tim.

The drawn curtains allowed little light into the dated living room. Mother's sittee loomed, vacant but waiting its queen's return. Huddled together over a circular table, Dad and Aunt Hettie whispered. Casey caught phrases. "Never would've believed she'd do such awful things." "Could have really hurt the girls." "Let you go to prison like that."

"Dad? Aunt Hettie? I'm so glad you're okay."

The pair startled apart from their conference.

"Casey!" Aunt Hettie crossed the room in three long strides and caught her by the shoulders. Tears glistened in Aunt Hettie's puffy, red-rimmed eyes. "I was so worried about you. About you all!" She stroked Casey's hair.

Casey cringed inwardly, uncomfortable but struggling to remain still and gracious. In a mousey voice, she said, "I'm sorry."

"For what?"

"If I'd have told the truth in the first place, you wouldn't have been sent to jail. Do not pass Go. Do not collect two hundred dollars."

Aunt Hettie squeezed Casey's arms, a gentle pressure. "Are you kidding? You did great, Casey. It was a misunderstanding's all. Now please stop rocking and don't fret."

"I didn't think they'd arrest you. I didn't want to get anyone in trouble."

Dad rubbed the bridge of his nose, his eyes pressed into resigned lines. "Of course you didn't."

Aunt Hettie placed her face before Casey's and forced eye contact. "And it's all okay now. You'll see."

"Where's Mom?"

Aunt Hettie and Dad exchanged uneasy looks with each other but excluded Casey.

After a brief, uncomfortable silence, Dad paced, hands clasped behind his back. "We're not sure where she's gotten to. But don't worry. She'll turn up soon. I'm sure."

Sure she will. Like a bad penny.

A breeze ruffled the curtains. They wafted like a warning, a spirit sure to appear.

"You have things you want to talk about. Right?" Her scrutiny implored until Aunt Hettie nodded. "Well, if it's okay with you, I'll take the kids to the store. We'll be back before bedtime, unless you call to tell me not to come home. You know, if Mom shows up. I'll keep them with me if she does."

Dad rested his hand against the wall near Casey. "Honey, you can't be frightened. This is your home. She's your mom."

Aunt Hettie threw her hands above her head. "Really? That's what I'm talking about. Of course she can be afraid." She motioned toward the kitchen. "They're all scared. And they should be."

Words strangled through Dad's tortured throat. "She's their mother. My wife."

"I know. She's my sister. And I love her. I do. But our focus has to be on the safety of the kids."

Casey cleared her throat. "Any idea where she is?"

Aunt Hettie offered a wobbly smile. "The police are looking for her, and the hospital's alerted."

Veins pulsed in Dad's temple. "You make her sound like a criminal. She's an ill woman. Frightened. And alone."

Aunt Hettie ran a hand down Casey's arm. "Don't worry, honey. They'll find her and get her to the hospital for treatment. You'll see. Everything will be okay. Please stop swaying."

Casey stiffened her muscles to stop. "I'll just be off with the kids, then. Call me if she shows up, okay? If she's here, tell me where to take the kids."

Dad sighed. "Bring the kids home, Casey. I want them to sleep in their own beds."

Aunt Hettie's head whipped toward Dad. "Damn it! If you won't let the little ones stay with me until this is resolved, then I'll stay here. I'll sleep in Casey's bed." She did a double take and softened her tone. "If you don't mind, of course, Casey."

"Not at all. It would be a great idea, I think."

Dad's jaw muscles pulsed.

The hardwood flooring creaked beneath Casey as she rocked. She forced words into the charged silence. "Well, then, you two work out those details while I stop by the mall. Be back soon."

Aunt Hettie ignored Dad's glare and waved goodbye. "Try to have fun. Love you."

"I love you both."

Casey joined her friends and siblings in the kitchen. "Let's take a little drive. If that's okay with you, Tim?"

He motioned toward the door with a theatrical bow. "After you."

CHAPTER THIRTY-ONE:
MALL MADNESS

Malcolm buckled himself into his booster seat as Rachel and Deirdre buckled up on either side of him.

"Where to?" Tim started the engine of Casey's car.

Casey clicked her seatbelt into place. "The Mall."

Rachel squealed. "Really? Oh, I love the Mall."

Deirdre muttered, "Never would've saw that coming."

Tim chuckled. "Do you want me to swing by campus and drop you off first?"

Malcolm wrapped his arms around Deirdre's middle. "No way! She wants to stay with us." The loving gaze he lavished on her put puppy dogs to shame. "You do want to stay with us, right?"

She snorted a little laugh. "Yeah, I'll come." She ruffled his hair, and he rested his head against her shoulder.

What the Westingham Mall lacked in active storefronts, it made up for with quirky charm. Craft guilds set up tables along the perimeters to display handcrafted goods. A group of local writers called The Nomadic Wordsters peddled books and hosted writing seminars. The Sportsmen's Association of Western PA demonstrated tracking and identification techniques, and appropriately positioned beside them, a local health agency handed out brochures and offered screenings to identify the dangers of tick-borne Lyme disease.

Rachel ooh'ed and ahh'ed over a fashion window display at a popular store.

Malcolm pointed to the games store. "I wish I had that system. My friends play together all the time. But I can't."

Tim snatched up Casey's hand and squeezed as they passed the lingerie store.

Deirdre followed, an observant shadow to their progress.

Casey led them into an electronics store and pointed to a display of pre-paid no-contract phones. She pointed to a row she could afford. "Pick one, Rach."

"Really?" Rachel's face burst with joy. "A phone?"

Malcolm frowned. "Do you need a new phone, Casey?"

"No, Rachel needs one."

Rachel squealed and pushed buttons on the nearest.

Casey touched Rachel's shoulder. "For emergencies, though. Not for every little thing. You'll only have so many minutes a month."

Rachel collected herself, but euphoria bubbled below the facade of decorum. "Of course." She glanced at her sister, hopeful. "But can I use it to call my friends now and then, too?"

"As long as you understand the minutes. This is for

emergencies."

For a long time, Rachel weighed every option and discussed each phones' virtues and shortcomings with a salesclerk named Chuck.

Malcolm grew bored. "Can I go to the games store, please? It's right over there."

"No, stay here with me. Surely Rachel won't be much longer."

But Rachel began to giggle and batted her eyes at Chuck, and Malcolm groaned. "Come on, Rachel. Just pick one already. Ugh." He slumped over a display of screen protectors.

Deirdre chuckled. "I can take him, if that's okay with you, Casey."

Malcolm perked up. "Please, please, please! I'll be good. I promise."

Deirdre smirked. "Besides, you can pretty much see the games store from here."

Casey hesitated. "I'd really rather…"

Rachel compared camera options with a loud, "Oh, this has filters built in!"

Casey sighed. "Okay. But behave yourself. Do you understand me?"

Malcolm's rapid nod sent his fine hair flying. Deirdre straightened, stiff as a soldier. "Yes ma'am. I will protect him with my life." Malcolm seized her hand, and the pair marched to their destination, Malcolm chattering about his friends' games as they went.

Tim slipped a hand around Casey's waist and whispered into her ear, "Is everything okay? At home, I mean?"

Casey shrugged. "Sort of. My Mom's missing."

Tim's grip tightened a bit. "Missing?"

Casey swallowed. "Police are alerted."

"Are you, I mean, should you be worried?" His gaze swept their surroundings as though expecting the appearance of her mother from behind a display.

"I am. Worried. A bit afraid. I don't think Mom's truly dangerous, but I know she needs help. If she'd get that, she'd be better. But who's to say she won't do something stupid with the kids in the meantime. That's why I'm getting this phone for Rachel."

Tim squeezed Casey to him. "That's smart. Besides, I don't think I've ever seen Rachel so happy."

As if in answer to his statement, Rachel twirled around the aisle with her chosen phone. When Casey paid for it, Rachel's montage of "thank you, thank you, thank you," grew annoying.

"Remember, this is bought for emergencies."

"I know, but I can't wait to show my friends!" Rachel hugged Casey again.

"Let's get your brother and Deirdre."

Malcolm held Deirdre's hand outside the games store. Both looked pale and confused.

Malcolm pulled Deirdre to greet them. "Casey, I saw a lady who looked like you, but I knowed it wasn't you because you don't smile like that." His wide-eyed expression conveyed fear. He whispered, "It was like at the hospital."

Deirdre nodded. "It was weird. She stood in the doorway and stared at us, all creepy-like." She shuddered.

Cold seized Casey. "Did she say anything?"

They both shook their heads. Deirdre said, "No, just stood and stared and smiled. Real creepy."

Rachel scanned the nearly empty halls. "Don't see anyone. Which way did she go?"

Malcolm pointed.

Tim narrowed his eyes in that direction. "Sounds like you might have a doppelganger, Casey."

CHAPTER THIRTY-TWO:
DOUBLE DOUBLE

Casey furrowed her brow. "A what?"

"A doppelganger. I've heard of them." Deirdre's eyes glinted with unmistakable interest. "Dr. Krochalis talked about them in Germanic folklore."

"I heard about them in Dr. Bridge's deviant psychology class. Doppelganger Effect," He noticed Deirdre glance away and mutter "Bridges," and cleared his throat. "But I think the psychological condition is inspired by the folklore." He paused. "Can you tell us about it, Deirdre?"

Deirdre's glance flicked up, almost hopeful.

Malcolm tugged her hand. "Yeah, I don't know what a doppelthingy is."

Deirdre straightened a bit. "It's a double. A replica of a person. Some say seeing one is a portent of death."

Rachel yelped, "Death?" and Malcolm's eyes widened.

Tim cleared his throat and knelt close to the kids. "It's an old legend, not real. It just means there's someone who looks like Casey walking around."

Rachel rested a hand on Tim's arm. "Wait, there's a website about finding celebrity doubles. Did you know there's a man from the Civil War who looks just like that actor from 'Ghost Rider?'" She cocked a mischievous smile. "Someone online said he's a vampire."

A growing prickle of cold, like ice melting along her spine, put Casey on alert. The conversation shrunk to a buzz as gooseflesh raised along her arms, and her stomach threatened to reject her last meal, which would have been sips of coffee with Jaimie instead of lunch. "Oh no," she whispered, but with everyone's attention focused on the kids, nobody heard.

Malcolm's voice broke through the drone, but his words didn't quite register. "That girl didn't look like Casey a whole bunch, though. She was scary. Casey's not scary." He released Deirdre's hand and sought his sister's. He scrutinized her face and whispered, "Casey, are you okay?"

Unaware of her brother's gentle concern, Casey sought the source of the discomfort, eyes darting in a frantic volley.

"Casey?" The weight of Tim's hand did not deter her search.

A soft moan broke from her lips. "No..."

Rachel's voice sounded shrill, near hysterics. "Are you okay, Casey? What's happening to her?"

Casey broke free from Malcolm and Tim and ran toward the problem, the soul in search of release. Tears streamed along her blazing cheeks to wet her hair.

A well-dressed young woman lay crumpled in a restroom corridor, purse contents and shopping bags strewn across the hall. A bottle of opioids speckled a new lime-green sweater and dressy blouse.

Casey skidded to a stop by her side, pleading in vain.

Foam bubbled from the woman's lips. Her eyes lolled like a broken doll's in their red-rimmed sockets. A pungent tang lingered like a fatal perfume about the woman who couldn't be much older than Casey.

Casey moaned louder and hunched closer to the departing woman. "No, hold on! I'll call for help." Her hands trembled as she fumbled with her phone while the soul of the young woman flutter, delicate as butterfly wings, frantic for release.

Tim knelt beside her and whispered close to her ear. "I've got it. I'll call 911."

Without a way to stem the time of grief, tears, snot, and agonized cries ripped through Casey. She forced words through her anguish. "Please. Don't let the kids see."

He pulled Casey into his lap, warm protection, a safe place to mourn. "Don't worry," he whispered. "Deirdre's got them, and she won't let them out of her sight." She melted into his comfort and allowed sickening waves of grief to wash over her. He stroked her hair as he described the emergency to the operator.

CHAPTER THIRTY-THREE:
TOIL AND TROUBLE

They all remained silent on the return trips. The kids sniffed goodbyes, and Rachel's subdued "thank you for the phone" spoke of her concern.

Aunt Hettie reassured she'd remain at the house until Mom returned for treatment.

Back at the dorm building, Tim kissed the top of Casey's head. "Be safe, my darling. I'm guessing you're not hungry?"

Casey nodded, eyes downcast.

"It's all right. We'll have to try for dinner another time, okay?"

Casey nodded again.

Tim kissed her lips, soft as the passage of a spring sigh. He turned to Deidre. "It was nice to meet you. Thanks for looking out for our girl and her family. You're a good egg."

Deirdre gave him a fist bump. "You're not too bad yourself, you big galoot."

Tim waved as he departed for the men's dorm.

As ever after an encounter with the departing, fatigue riddled Casey's joints, and she stumbled a bit as she made her way inside.

"Easy there, sailor. You may be little, but I don't want to be carrying you up to the dorm." She slipped an arm under Casey's to add support and guided. "Of course you know, you're going to have to explain what the hell happened at the mall eventually. Got it? But first we'll get some sleep."

The RA waited in their hall, arms crossed, grim expression darkening her delicate features. "So, you're back. Good. We need to talk."

Both Casey and Deirdre stiffened.

Deirdre extricated herself. "What's up, boss?"

The R.A. motioned with a jerk of her chin toward their door. "We'll talk inside." She glared around at the closed doors. "Less prying ears."

Casey followed the women into her dorm room. Her ears still rang with her own wails, hollowed and empty. She sat on her bed, stiff and mechanical.

The R.A. pulled a laptop from her shoulder bag, opened it, and clicked on a file. "This is from the hallway security camera from the time of the break-in." She stepped back to allow the roommates a clear view.

On screen, Casey emerged from their room and shoved Deirdre's medicine bottles into her red coat pockets. She smacked lips darkened with the lipstick used to write a message on their mirror and smiled directly into the security camera before slipping her room key into the neighbor's lock and gaining admittance.

Deirdre paled, eyes narrowed, nostrils flared. "You?" Her voice rose. "You took my medicine? You broke into the other rooms?" Her arms flailed as she rounded on

Casey who remained too still and stunned to react. "Why? I thought we were friends!"

Casey's mind jumbled. Incoherent sounds squeaked through her lips. Tears slicked her vision on the computer screen.

Deirdre's chest heaved as she struggled for control. She addressed the R.A. "So what happens now?"

Does she really believe I did this? Of course, why wouldn't she?

The R.A. re-crossed her arms over her bosom. "Of course we have to take this up with the Dean in the morning."

"I can't stay here with her. Not after this." Deirdre pointed to the computer.

Casey stood on shaking legs. "I'll go. You don't have to share a room with me."

The R.A. grabbed her arm. "Hold it right there. You've been caught stealing. I could call campus police and have them lock you up for the night."

"Please don't." Casey gulped and pulled her thoughts together. "I'll go and promise to meet you at the Dean's office in the morning."

The R.A. frowned. "Be there by nine."

Casey nodded. "Promise."

Casey clutched her blanket, pillow, and bag to her chest like a child's security items and exited. People peered from behind doors as she passed, and their whispers followed like rustles of a breeze through emerging grasses.

CHAPTER THIRTY-FOUR:
IN THE DEAN'S OFFICE

Laden with a bag of belongings and clutching her bedding before her, Casey shambled to her car. She dumped everything inside and collapsed onto the seat. The spring air did nothing to invigorate her sensibilities. Everything swirled in her mind, a confusion of leering smiles, troubling words, and death rattles.

She formed a cocoon of her blanket and hoped to bury her worries beneath a pillow of oblivion. Her last thought before she set her phone alarm, turned off its ringer, and drifted off to an uneasy sleep was "Deirdre must hate me now."

She woke, shivering, cramped, and aching before the alarm sounded. She picked out fresh clothes and toiletries and shoved them into her backpack. *Maybe I can duck in and use the washroom before my appointment with the Dean.*

A low fog prowled the campus, but birds sang of merry returns and private joys. Swaths of hyacinth and daffodils popped above the ankle-deep fog, lending their heady perfume to smells of turned soil.

Somewhere by the lake, a kilted man played bagpipes.

Casey tidied up without encountering anyone. She applied a thin layer of makeup to cover her fatigue, gathered her belongings, and steeled her resolve. *Time to face the dragon.*

The corridor to Dr. Julia Rosen's office stretched much longer than she remembered. The secretary grimaced a "good morning." She swept Casey with a tight-lipped appraisal. "Are you expected?"

Casey couldn't meet the woman's brilliant eyes. Her nod tossed her hair over her face, and she muttered, "I believe so." Nobody else sat in the chairs. *At least we won't prolong this agony.*

"Are you waiting for someone else to arrive?"

Casey nodded.

The secretary pointed to the coffee station. "Help yourself, if you want."

Casey added several packets of sugar and half a cup of milk to her cup before adding the bitter brown liquid. Each swallow warmed her throat but could not remove the chill of dread. *Will they boot me? What can I possibly say to defend myself? Nobody in their right mind would believe I have a doppelganger.* Sunlight streamed through a stained-glass window topper, casting beautiful patterns along the polished wood. Casey ran her fingers through the light as she had her last visit to the Dean's office. She'd wondered then if she'd be chucked out of school. Now, though, she felt its certainty heavy as a millstone about her neck. Or a noose about to tighten.

"Good. You're here." The R.A. shifted her shoulder bag to free a hank of her bushy hair from the strap. "Didn't think you'd show. Well, let's get on with it."

She turned to the secretary. "Mrs. Wellesley, we need to see Dean Rosen, please. Right away, if possible."

After she rang the Dean, Secretary Wellesley motioned them inside. "She's waiting for you. Don't be long, though. She has an appointment arriving at 10:45."

The R.A. glanced at Casey. "I can't think this will take long." She patted her bag. "The evidence is pretty concise."

Casey's stomach lurched. With funerary precision, she dragged herself in the R.A.'s wake to stand before the vast mahogany desk and impressive framed credentials of Dean Rosen. Dr. Rosen rested her chin on steepled fingers when they entered.

The R.A. stepped up to the desk, stiff with officiousness. "I don't mean to take up much of your time, Dean Rosen, but this freshman broke into several dorm rooms and caused mischief. I knew you'd want to deal with the matter personally."

"I see." Dean Rosen motioned to a pair of chairs. "Ms. Blanco, Ms. Adams, please take seats and explain what happened."

Casey's trembling caused the little coffee remaining in her cup to slosh onto her bookbag when she took a seat.

Instead of sitting, Ms. Blanco removed her computer from her bag. "There were several break-ins on our floor, and the hallway footage captured the culprit." She pressed play, and the incriminating evidence rolled for the Dean.

Dean Rosen glanced at Casey for a moment before addressing Ms. Blanco. "How many rooms were invaded?"

"All of them on that corridor."

Casey regretted drinking the coffee. It sloshed in her stomach and threatened to make a reappearance.

The R.A. puffed out her chest. "I know I should have called campus police, but I thought you might want to deal with this personally."

"Just so." Dean Rosen leaned closer to the screen and squinted. She lifted her glasses and renewed her scrutiny.

A slight commotion outside the office preceded a loud knock which echoed through the room. Without acknowledgement, the door burst open. In rushed Deirdre pursued by a harried Ms. Wellesley. "I'm sorry, Dr. Rosen." She straightened her rumpled blouse. "She refused to wait like a civilized person."

"I'm sorry to be so rude," Deirdre gasped. "I had to see you." She locked eyes with Casey. "Good, you're still here. I was afraid I'd missed you."

Dr. Rosen's raised eyebrows and quivering mouth betrayed more than surprise. She dismissed Ms. Wellesley. "I assume this student has something to present in relation to this matter. Thank you."

Ms. Wellesley returned to her desk with a last glare of reproach for all the students.

When the door clicked behind her, Dr. Rosen motioned to the bank of leather chairs before her desk. When Deirdre took the one beside Casey, Dean Rosen asked, "Well, what insight have you to offer?"

"I'm Casey Adam's roommate, ma'am, and I've been thinking about this all night. Couldn't sleep a wink. Something about that security tape bothered me. See, I think I know Casey pretty well, and I know she wouldn't break into rooms or loot people's stuff. She's not that kind of person."

Ms. Blanco laughed and pointed to her computer. "Are you crazy? You only just met her, and you saw her guilt with your own eyes!"

Deirdre leapt to the monitor. "Play it."

The self-assured R.A. complied.

"There! You see, Casey doesn't even like to make eye contact, let alone knowingly look into a camera and smile. And look how she walks. This person's all cocky, striding along the halls like she owns the place. Have you ever watched Casey? She scuttles along the edges like a little mouse afraid to bump into anyone." She tapped the desk. "That's not Casey. It's an imposter."

Ms. Blanco's mouth hung slack. "You're mental."

"No, I'm not. Well, not about this, anyway. At the mall the other day, I saw a woman who looked a lot like Casey. I think this look-alike is stalking Casey." Deirdre took a deep breath. "I know it's improbable..."

"But improbability dogs Ms. Adam's footsteps, does it not?" Dr. Rosen replaced her glasses. "Was anything stolen, Ms. Blanco?"

The R.A. flipped over a page on her yellow tablet. "A bag of dice, a bottle of rum, and" she considered Casey and Deirdre, "her medicine and a lipstick," she indicated Deirdre, then tipped her head toward Casey, "and her winter jacket." She narrowed her eyes at Casey. "Of course, since she did the breaking in, I guess it's not missing at all."

The Dean closed the monitor and pushed it toward Ms. Blanco. "Thank you for bringing this to me. Excellent work. Please ask the women in your care to use common sense and lock their doors. I'll take it from here."

Ms. Blanco ogled. "You don't mean to say you believe she's got some evil twin breaking into dorm rooms, do you?"

"I'll have to explore the possibilities. Thank you, Ms. Blanco."

The R.A. closed her gaping mouth, gathered her things while she muttered "unbelievable," and left without another word.

"Ms. Adams, did you break into your classmates' dorm rooms?"

Casey swallowed hard and shook her head. "No, Ma'am, I didn't."

"Did you take your roommate's medicines?"

Tears spilled over Casey's lids. "No. Deirdre's my friend."

Deirdre squeezed her hand. Tears danced in her eyes, too. "Please believe her, Dr. Rosen. I know how it looks, but Casey didn't do it. Even if the camera thinks she did."

Dr. Rosen tapped the desktop and scrutinized them. "This is a peculiar predicament we find ourselves in. There is film of what appears to be you, Ms. Adams, leaving the scene of a crime. Few would be astute enough to note the differences in mannerisms between you and the screen person as your friend here, so we're dealing with possible mistrust and worse. And while Ms. Blanco is a good Resident Advisor, and she tries for discretion, she is not above sharing some gossip on occasion, especially if she feels the situation is wrongly handled." Dr. Rosen sighed and, as though she'd made a decision, pushed a button on her desk phone. "Bernice, please see if you can catch Ms. Blanco, the young woman who just left here."

"Yes, Dr. Rosen."

"Run along now, you two. I will talk with Ms. Blanco."

Casey felt faint with relief. She all but bolted from her seat, intent upon leaving before the Dean changed her mind.

"Ms. Adams."

Casey froze. *I knew it was too good to be true.* She turned with trepidation, her voice more quivery than gelatin on a spoon. "Yes, Dr. Rosen?"

"I know it's hard for you, but do try to stay away from trouble." With a hint of a smile and a nod of her head, she dismissed Casey.

Casey dropped her chin and slumped from the room. *Like I try to get into trouble.*

CHAPTER THIRTY-FIVE: ARCHAIC KNOWLEDGE

Outside, chilled air pinked their cheeks. Clouds gathered overhead, as though to listen in on their conversation.

Deirdre bumped into Casey, sending her skipping a couple of steps from the path. "That went better than I thought."

"You came to help."

"Look, Casey, I'm sorry about what I said yesterday." Deirdre chewed her lip. "Really sorry. I was confused and upset, especially after we talked about... about why I have those pills."

"It is pretty confusing. I'm not sure what's happening, but I think I know someone to ask."

"Oh? Who's that?"

"Dr. Krochalis. She's really knowledgeable about weird stuff. I think having a double would be considered weird, don't you?"

Deirdre nodded. "Yeah, it's pretty messed up. Is that where you're going now?"

Casey nodded.

"Mind if I tag along?"

Casey smiled at her. "I'd be glad of your company."

They descended the stairs toward Professor Krochalis' building. Birdsong punctuated their journey, a reflection of the relief Casey felt. "I thought I was going to be kicked out for sure."

Deirdre clamped her jaw tight and swallowed hard. Color rose in her cheeks, and tears sparkled. She whispered, "I'm so sorry."

Casey studied her friend's face and chewed her lip. "Why on earth are you sorry?"

Deirdre bumped Casey with her hip. "You weirdo." She wiped a tear from her cheek. "I never should have doubted you. I knew you didn't steal from me, but I guess I was so upset that my - medicine - was gone, and you knew why I had it. In the back of my mind, I blamed you, although I knew you didn't do anything. I knew it, and I let you take the blame." She whispered, "You could have been expelled or charged." She sniffed. "I wasn't being a good friend."

Casey furrowed her brow and considered her words. "You rushed to the Dean's office to defend me. And you're missing classes to see if Dr. Krochalis knows anything about this strange double thing."

A deep male voice interrupted. "Strange double thing? What mischief have you gotten yourself into this time, Ms. Adams?" The head of the Psychology department, Dr. Bridges, tipped his head to them. "I don't believe you're schizophrenic, so..." He removed his glasses and swiped them with a flourish of his monogrammed handkerchief. "Are you reading Dostoevsky's novella? Or..." When he replaced his glasses, his eyes sparkled. "Are you experiencing a parietal-lobe-inspired delusion?"

Dr. Bridges leaned against the entry, lean and attractive in his patched-elbowed sports jacket and blue jeans, eyebrows raised, awaiting a response.

Casey gulped, heat infiltrating her jaw lines and cheeks. "Um..."

Dr. Bridges' eyebrows raised higher. A bird's trill interrupted the awkward silence.

Deirdre raised her hands and smiled. "Goodness, you're free with the diagnoses, but how reassuring." She rested a hand on Casey's shoulder and ignored Casey's stiffened response. "Casey, you're not schizophrenic." She swiped her hand across her forehead and flicked away pretended perspiration. "Guess we can continue on to find Professor Krochalis who you were looking for now." She gave Casey a gentle shove toward the destination.

Dr. Bridges shook his head, laughed, and turned to leave. "I dare say Jeanne will be pleased to see you and your affrontable new companion, Ms. Adams. Good luck with whatever you're embroiled in. I look forward to the intriguing tale." With another chuckle, he walked away.

Deirdre snorted. "Who was that smug man?"

Casey struggled to find her voice. "Dr. Bridges, the head of the psychology department."

"Wait. That's Bridges?" She turned to stare at the man's swagger. She pointed at him. "You wanted me to talk to that ass about my problems? Oh, Casey." Deirdre shook her head, a sardonic smile plastered on her lips.

Casey's voice piped out, small and timid. "He's really knowledgeable."

Another snort. "If so, he sure knows it. Puffed up

priss."

Casey frowned at Dr. Krochalis' office door. "He and Dr. K. are my favorite professors."

"No offense, Casey." Deirdre giggled. "He's just so full of himself. I have a class with Dr. K. I hope Krochalis isn't such a blow hard as that man."

From behind came a high-pitched voice. "There's always hope."

Casey and Deirdre jumped in surprise.

Dr. Krochalis tapped a polka dot bow-topped ballet slipper. "Excuse me." She brushed through to unlock her office door. "Coming?"

Casey and Deirdre exchanged wide-eyed looks before following her inside.

"Dr. Krochalis, this is my roommate, Deirdre."

"Pleasure." Dr. Krochalis' pressed lips denoted anything but. "So, what seems to be the trouble today? Angels whispering in the apple blossoms? Imps in the impatiens?"

"No, actually, have you ever heard of a Doppelganger?"

"A double walker, Ms. Adams. Yes. I've heard of them. Why?"

"How does a person get rid of one?"

"Hm, I don't think they do. In fact, most cultures believe to see one predicts the death of the person in question." She grabbed a book from her overstuffed shelves and turned to the index. She ran her finger along until she found her entry and paged to it. "Here we are. Doppelganger is the German term for a Double Walker. Some believe it is a demon taking the guise of another to cause mischief. In some cultures powerful magicians summon these chameleons to harm their enemies. There are a number of historic mentions of doubles. Hm. A Sci-fi writer suggests seeing a doppelganger may be an instance where time rips, and a person sees himself from a different time."

"That's interesting, professor, but what I need to know is how do I - um, how does someone - defeat one."

Dr. Krochalis read, her color rising in her cheeks. "That's tricky. If it was a summoned demon, the magician who performed the magic could be forced to dispel the summons. Many sources suggest avoidance, because confronting the doppelganger causes death to one of the twins." She pointed to a pre-Raphaelite painting. "If it is a malicious spirit, though, the usual precautions should do the job."

Deirdre tapped her foot. "Standard precautions? Like what? Call Ghostbusters? I don't think they pay calls to podunk towns like the Ol' Nor'Eastern campus community."

Dr. Krochalis bristled. "There are paranormal investigators in the area, but I'm suggesting something like religious protections, if there is faith behind them. Salt is said to trap or hold ghosts at bay. Iron harms some. There are ways of trapping spirits and ways to guide them along to their next life." She stole a quick glance at Casey.

"I don't think this is a ghost, though. It doesn't feel trapped or frustrated." Casey stared at a crow outside Dr. Krochalis' window. The bird returned her scrutiny. "In fact, it feels purposeful and malicious."

"Maybe something caught the thing's attention. Like, maybe an ability it doesn't appreciate. This source suggests if a doppelganger can lead a soul astray, it can capture it. My thought is if something guided souls to their next life," She intensified her consideration of Casey, "that soul-helper would be a hindrance to the soul-snatcher."

"So, how does a soul-helper send a soul-snatcher on its way?"

Dr. Krochalis leaned close enough to the book to brush her nose against the page. "I don't see anything at the moment, but I'll keep reading. I'll let you know as soon as I discover something useful."

"Thanks. I appreciate your help." Casey turned to leave.

"Oh, Ms. Adams, did you know someone re-opened Lily's psychic shop? I wonder if the new manager might have a suggestion?"

"I'll check it out. Thank you again."

Deirdre followed Casey into the weak streams of buttery spring sunlight. "Who's Lily, and what's a psychic shop?"

Casey smiled at her. "Lily was one of Dr. Krochalis' old students. She organized the equinox ceremony last September, the one Jaimie, Tim, and I attended." *Among other people, Rom included.* A shudder ripped through her. "Lily died," *An invisible veil strangled her before my eyes, a heart attack or something.* She shook herself. "Her partner was arrested, so I guess her New Age shop was closed."

"So is that the next stop?"

"It's on my list of stops."

"Want company?"

Casey stopped mid-stride. "Company?"

"Yeah, me." Deirdre pointed to her chest and laughed. "Do you mind if I tag along?"

"I'm confused. Don't you have classes to attend?"

"Are you trying to get rid of me, or are you channeling my academic advisor? Besides, you have classes that you're missing, too, don't you?"

"I somehow don't think I'll be able to concentrate as long as there's a troublemaker wearing my face walking about."

"I get that. Let's go."

A zephyr caressed their skin as they negotiated the cobblestone pathways to the parking area.

"I have an idea." Casey unlocked the car. "Do you mind interviewing the shopkeeper at the New Age store while I run an errand just outside of town? I have to check on something, and time's running away today."

Deirdre's face fell for a moment. "Yeah, I guess I could do that."

"It would be a huge help." Casey rubbed her eyes and stifled a yawn. "Maybe we can get this done before sunset."

"Say, where did you sleep last night? I tried calling, but it went straight to voicemail."

Casey jolted. "Oh, I had my ringer off." She pulled the phone from her pant pocket. "Shoot, I missed calls from Tim, Jaimie, and you."

Deirdre pointed to Casey's shoulder. "You have a butterfly."

The now-familiar blue spots appeared as the insect opened its wings.

Casey smiled at it as she wound down her window. "Hello, friend. I doubt you want to join us. You probably have lots of butterfly pals waiting for you." She swiveled in her seat to allow the butterfly an escape, but the thing leaped to her cheek. At the touch of its tiny legs, agony for a lifetime lived without purpose wrung bitter tears from her. "Oh," she moaned and thumped her head against her steering wheel.

Deirdre's voice trembled. "Are you okay?" She gasped.

Several butterflied joined their companion and vied for her attention and touch. Dozens of velvety wings accosted and obscured Casey's sight. Miniature feet brought regrets and bittersweet joys. She lived through experiences beyond anything offered in her sheltered life. She knew the agony of addiction, the disbelief of a sudden end. Longing twisted within her like a coiled serpent prepared for a strike. A newborn's blurry-blue eyes blinked into her own, and her heart swelled with pride. Snow sprayed her face, icy bites against unprotected, bluing skin.

So many last moments relived through contact with jewel-bright messengers requiring Casey's tears to clear a path to the afterlife. As Casey spilled her private ocean for the benefit of the diminutive soul-conveyors, they fluttered into golden sunbeams, intent upon private purpose.

When the last butterfly left, Casey's ragged breathing calmed. In her stomach, a rock of regrets settled. Her vision blurred with tears and aches. She rested her head against the cool metal of the window track and sniffed until she could at last clear her eyes and face her own tasks.

"What the hell just happened?"

Casey startled. She'd forgotten Deirdre's presence, overwhelmed by an ambush of unbridled emotions not her own. Casey adjusted her mirror. Mascara left grey tracks over blotchy, swollen skin. She swiped with her index finger to remove the racoon effect. "I'm not entirely sure."

"Seriously, what the hell? You were crawling with butterflies and keening like an injured wolf!"

"I'm sorry. I guess they're souls hoping for release."

Deirdre's mouth fell open wider than her bulging eyes. She shivered and whispered, "Holy crap, girl. How often does this happen?"

Casey giggled, giddy with exhaustion. "I've never been jumped by butterflies before, actually. Don't think I want it to happen again, either." She rubbed the back of her neck. Her voice quivered. "Ever."

Deirdre exhaled loudly. "Damn, girl, I'm glad I'm not you."

CHAPTER THIRTY-SIX:
OFF TO ARKHAM

Casey collected herself before she drove to the New Age bookstore, grateful for Deirdre's quiet company.

When she pulled in, she allowed her head to flop onto the neck rest. "Thank you for doing this, Deirdre. See if you can find out how I can beat this thing trying to steal my face."

"I got you, girlfriend. I know what we need." She cocked her head to better view the storefront. "Just hope this hokey shop can give us some answers." She eyed Casey. "Where are you off to, anyway?"

Casey allowed her eyelids to slide shut. "I have to see if the facility heard anything from my mother." She pressed her lips tight to keep them from trembling. Her voice sounded small and hopeless. "I'm still afraid for my family."

"Lord, you have a lot on your plate. I don't know how you do it. Be careful, all right? I'll get as much information as I can about doppelgangers and that creepy stuff. You stay away from butterflies. I don't trust those buggers anymore."

Casey sniggered. "I'll keep an eye out." She opened

her eyes when her car door thudded closed and Deirdre waved from the shop door. "Off to Arkham, then," Casey announced to the empty car.

Inside the facility, the security staff subjected her to the standard entrance procedure. Present an I.D. Sign in. Pass through a metal detector and have her purse inspected. With a visitor badge that displayed her photograph and name taped to her shirt, a guard escorted Casey to the office of Dr. Keller, the psychiatrist who treated her mother.

Antiseptic vied with urine. They passed locked wards. At one, a disheveled woman thumped her fist against the reinforced glass in a monotonous rhythm. From behind another came sounds of mutters and a shriek. They turned down a hallway to the doctor's office.

"He's not in. Wait here. I'll check the logbook. Be right back." The guard's crisp uniform provided stark contrast to the clinical white of walls, floor, and ceiling, like an early bluebird lost in a snowy field.

Another set of footfalls and the clanking of a chain announced two guards, an orderly, and an inmate enroute through Casey's waiting spot. The guards strode with confidence, their charge a limp, stumbling scarecrow between them, while the orderly consulted charts. As they neared, the patient grew restless and struggled in their grip.

"Oh my, it's little Casey Contrary! Casey, look at me. Look!"

Casey flicked her gaze to his face. Beneath a scraggly beard and unkempt hair smirked her one-time associate, Rom. He'd lost weight, and dark grey bags gave his eyes a sunken, skeletal appearance. He grinned, a crooked, malicious expression.

"That's the girl who put me here. That's Casey. She's some kind of retard or something. Aren't you, Casey? I see you, Casey Adams. I remember."

"That's enough from you." The guards pulled him along the corridor, but Rom's head lulled, and he fixed Casey with a stare.

"Don't come to my room anymore. You hear me? I don't want to see you." His head flopped to the orderly. "I don't want her coming to visit me anymore. That girl right there. You see her, right? She was here the other day, remember? Well, I don't want her coming here again. I don't want to see you again, Casey Adams. You don't scare me. Don't come to see me again." Rom's conversational circle continued until the elevator doors closed.

Again? Was that doppelganger here, too, or is Rom raging?

Dr. Keller interrupted her musings. "Nice to see you again, Ms. Adams. How can I help you?"

"I wondered if you'd heard from my mother?"

"As I told you earlier, no. We've no idea where your mother's gone."

"Told me earlier? When?"

He raised his eyebrows. He spoke with measured intonations, as though afraid to upset her. "Yesterday, when we discussed your mother's disappearance. As I told you then, she was a self-admitted person. We could not hold her against her will. I will call your father if I hear from your mother." He placed a hand on Casey's shoulder to guide her toward the exit.

Casey shied from his touch. "Thank you, doctor. I appreciate your time." The way she'd bunched her eyebrows in the center of her forehead strained, and a headache prickled at the corners of her consciousness as she retraced her way through security, turned in her badge, and started her car's engine.

CHAPTER THIRTY-SEVEN:
SURPRISE ALLIES

By the time she reached the bookstore, Casey's resolve settled on her like a suit of armor. She punched her steering wheel. "I'm taking care of this doppelganger thing before it ruins my life." She checked her phone.

Shoot, I forgot the messages from Jaimie and Tim.

From Jaimie came, "I miss you! You didn't come for coffee. Is everything ok? BTW, look at the ceremony hill. Doesn't it look amazing? Do you think some poor saps are up there having another equinox ceremony? I may hike up there and check later, or do you think it would be a dawn thing since it's spring? I mean, when we went in the autumn, it was a sunset. In any case, let me know when we can get together. I miss you, Casey! Love you!"

Tim wrote, "The sun shines brighter when you're around. I've not seen your smile in too long. Can I take you to dinner? I can't wait to see you, gorgeous."

The phone cooled like a balm where Casey rested it against her forehead a minute before she stepped into the crisp afternoon air. The shop bell jangled its proclamation. Inside looked crowded with new agisms. Baskets overflowed with feathers. Light-catching crystals hung from cords and chains. Bookshelves sagged beneath their eclectic burdens. A tan cat bumped its head against Casey's shin and rubbed against her. Its purr rumbled.

A woman about Casey's age peeked around the edge of one of a pair of overstuffed chintz chair in the reading corner. Her long locks spilled nearly to the ground. "Hi! Welcome, and merry met! I'm Sunbeam." She made a relaxed wave toward the cat. "Jinx likes you. Means you must be on the road to ascension. Good for you!" She disappeared from view, facing away from Casey, but her voice trilled, "Let me know if I can be of help to you." She rested her bare feet on a coffee table.

Deirdre smiled over the top of the other chair. "Wait, Sunny, that's the girl I told you about. Casey, Sunny runs this place."

"Oh, you're the target of the double-dealer, are you?" Sunny stood. "I'm so sorry. That sucks. But don't worry. We figured it out."

Thick plumes of incense worsened Casey's headache, but she focused on the shopkeeper. "Figured what out?"

"How to summon the thing. And Casey guess what? Sunny said she'd help!" Deirdre placed a hand on Sunny's shoulder.

Sunny patted Deirdre's hand and bumped against her, playful and flirtatious. "This one's a good friend to you, little lady."

"I know she's a good friend, thank you." Casey rubbed her temples. "What do we have to do to trap the thing or send it where it can't hurt anyone ever again?"

Sunny's dreamy smile slipped a little. "Let's start with summoning it, and we can go from there."

Deirdre pointed to a bag beside her chair. "Sunny's letting us borrow the stuff we need."

"That's really nice of you." W*hy be so nice to a stranger, though*? "Thank you."

As though reading Casey's thoughts, Sunny declared, "I see auras, and I could tell from Deirdre's that something dire stalked her. I want to help."

The cat wandered behind the counter, tail high as noon.

Deirdre slung the bag over her shoulder. "What do you see in Casey's aura?"

Sunny's expression grew vacant, and her voice drifted, misty as the incense smoke. "Gold for love, lots of love, and silver, a guide." She closed her eyes. "No wonder the demon targeted you. It must hate you."

"Why would it hate her, Sunny?"

"She steals its food. It sups on confusion. She likes order. It thrives when souls are lost. She sends them on their path through the veil." Sunny's long lashes rested near her high cheekbones, as though she'd fallen asleep standing.

"Is that what you do, Casey?"

Casey shrugged. "I'm not sure what I do, but I know it's time to go. Do you think we can summon this thing today?"

Sunny blinked as though waking from a nap. "Maybe. Every day holds magic, but today is the spring equinox. That means our chances are greater."

"Great. Let's go." Deirdre led them from the shop.

"Protect the place, Jinxy. Be back as soon as I can." Sunny flipped the sign to "closed" and locked up. She moved her hand across the door's seal and muttered a string of words.

Deirdre leaned against the wall, arms crossed, to watch. "What're you doing?"

"A spell. Keeps away robbers." Sunny flipped her hair over her shoulder until it tumbled *en masse* to the small of her thin waist. "I'm good at spells." She smiled and followed to Casey's car.

CHAPTER THIRTY-EIGHT:
TEAMWORK

"We need someplace quiet and away from too much interference to do this summoning." Sunny spun around the campus. "Any ideas, ladies?"

Casey gasped. What Jaimie had referred to as the ceremony hill glowed, the trees bright with white. Not snow. An abundance of blossoms coated the dark branches.

Sunny gasped. "It's beautiful."

"Nobody would see us there. The path to the top's this way." As Casey guided them, pale pink petals floated on whispered breezes.

Mud made the steep paths slippery. Deirdre offered her arms to Casey and Sunny, sturdy and sure-footed in combat boots. Chirps, songs, buzzes, and rustles around them told of wildlife luxuriating in warmer temperatures. Birds flitted with materials for nests. Squirrels scolded, silvery tails a-twitch, noses a-twitter.

When they reached the clearing where last autumn Casey joined Jaimie and members of the band Stages of Grief for an ill-advised ceremony, no evidence of animals or birds disturbed an eerie quiet. Then, skeletal trees had loomed overhead like a ceiling of disapproving giants.

Now, though, the trees bristled with life.

Casey whispered, "Will this do?" Somehow, it felt right.

Sunny's large eyes widened as she nodded. She and Deirdre unpacked candles, a dark-framed mirror, an ornate box, and a silver chain from the bag.

"We'll need to prepare the trap. Double Walkers are sometimes spirits." She shook a container of pink, large-grained salt. "This will protect us if this one's a ghost double." She removed a plastic bottle with a gold cross atop. "This is in case the thing's a demon, though. Salt will help, but we'll need a bit more protection if it's a demon. I'm hoping you can trap it in this mirror, but if not, I brought this box."

The glint from the cross dazzled Casey. "How do you know the difference?"

"A ghost double might have an important message for you, or be here to warn of bad luck to come." Sunny ducked her head and whispered, "Like, it might be here to tell you of your death."

Deirdre snorted. "What?" Her wide eyes searched Casey's face.

Sunny cleared her throat. "Of course, a demon might have other reasons for imitating someone. A way to create discord, you know? But then, many demons are excellent imitators. They mimic voices and spread lies."

Casey thought of the being's changes at the hospital. "So, let's go with the demon theory. I've seen this thing look like a whole bunch of people. But why would it pick on me?"

Sunny shrugged. "Why does anyone do anything they do?"

The sun slipped into a spectacular sunset brilliant with pastels of pink and turquoise, violet and salmon. Sunny motioned for Casey to sit before the mirror. Her voice buzzed like a bumblebee, a quiet tickle in Casey's ear. "Let your mind go blank. You're connected to this thing, so you should be able to see it within the scrying glass."

Candlelight flickered and reflected along its surface. Casey's reflection showed weariness in dark circles and paler than usual skin. The staples in her scalp itched, and her head throbbed in time to her heartbeat. Perhaps a trick of the candlelight and the sunset, but Casey's outline blurred and wavered.

A rustle, then another, told of someone's approach.

"Hey, who's out there?" Deirdre's voice barked like a guard dog.

A little voice said, "Is that my fwiend?"

"Malcolm?" Casey's pulse pounded faster than the spring-swollen streams. *What's he doing here?* Search as she might, she could not see into the shadows to find her brother.

"Don't get too far ahead," came a worried warning.

Rachel, too? How'd they get here? How'd they know to look for me way up here?

A thick voice growled, "Both of you need to mind your mother."

It was as though entire rivers of frigid ice water washed over Casey. *No. Not now. Not Mom.*

Malcolm emerged from the burgeoning underbrush first, followed by a harried-looking Rachel. He ran headlong in a flying embrace that sent Casey sprawling. He whispered into her ear, "I knew I'd find you."

Murmurs from nearby told of Deirdre and Sunny's continued efforts, and something flashed behind the tree trunks, a fleet-footed person with hair streaming behind.

Casey struggled to her feet, hand on Malcolm's head. Solid and smelling of cookies, Malcolm was no phantom but a vulnerable little person. *I can't let anything bad happen to him! Or to Rachel.* Desperation made her voice shrill. "What are you doing here?"

Rachel's lip trembled. She hugged her arms about her thin body. "Mom's back, Casey. She said you told her to meet you here."

Chills intensified. "I never said that."

Between huffed breaths, Mom's sultry voice accused, "Still a liar, are you?" Mom stepped from the growing gloom surrounding them. Her low-cut green blouse allowed a clear view of her ample bosom's rise and fall. "I'd hoped you might grow out of the habit, but I see that in this, as in so many things, you disappoint."

Casey's voice trembled like a child's. "I don't lie."

"Ah, then how did I know to find you here, in this obscure location?"

Casey's pulse raced, and sweat slicked her forehead despite the nip in the air. "There's this doppelganger thing..." *Great. Now I sound like a crazy person.*

A cold, laughing voice from near the mirror interrupted. "Because I wanted you to find it, of course."

Casey spun to face the speaker. Same pale face as

her own. Same blonde waves. Same dark-fringed, pale eyes. Dressed in Casey's red coat, the doppelganger stood straighter, though, and looked on boldly, a malicious hardness to her expression. It cast no shadow and walked with the silent grace of a snake.

"What are you playing at now, girl?" Mom's face darkened, and a scowl pulled her lips toward her paunchy jawline. "A new trick to get your poor mother in trouble?"

The doppelganger's grin sent fresh shivers up Casey's spine. Casey yelled at the thing. "Why? Why would you lure my mother and sister and brother here?"

The doppelganger's smile slid askew. "I only asked for the mother. The children are an unlooked-for pleasure. I asked her here for a simple reason. To allow her to see your destruction." She reached toward Casey, voice thick with malevolence. "She deserves that, don't you think?"

Casey stepped away from the touch with the acumen of one long accustomed to avoidance of contact. "No, I don't. She deserves love and respect. She requires care." Casey glanced at her mother. "She's dealing with some tough things and needs a little help is all."

The not-Casey threw back its head and laughed. "Your mother hates you, idiot. She wishes you'd never been born. I for one agree with her and feel strongly that her hatred should be rewarded. It is a balm to all who thrive on chaos and revenge, as my brethren and I do."

The not-Casey narrowed her eyes. "But why is it you're standing here, bold as brass, and not collapsed in a gibbering heap at the mere sight of me?" Her breath stank of sulfur, and an ill-definition clouded the lines of her cheeks, as though an artist neglected the line work.

Casey fixated on their lack. "You know, up close, you don't actually look like me."

The not-Casey chuckled. "I look more like you than you will ever achieve. I am your essence. I personify your soul." She wrapped the coat around her thin body like a hug.

Casey frowned. "What does that even mean? Are you a ghost? A demon? Do you have a soul? And why would you bother with me or mine?"

With aggressive strides, the not-Casey closed the gap between them until she almost stood atop Casey's feet. "It means, you dolt, that when you look at me, you should see your failings and know your time on this earth has come to an end. Now look at me. Look into my eyes instead of allowing your vision to skate about."

With a rough hand, the doppelganger gripped Casey's chin and pulled.

Its eyes resembled dull chips of ice, and fogginess of its features bothered Casey.

"You really don't look much like me at all."

The not-Casey's mouth dropped open. "You've got to be kidding me! I look precisely like you." It pulled off Casey's jacket and tossed it. *My missing jacket! You did steal it.* It rattled when it hit the ground.

The doppelganger spat, "And why the hell are you still alive? Your puny mind should have collapsed beneath the enormity of this situation. Your sins should have crushed your spirit. Your shortcomings left you with nothing to live for. How are you standing here with a beating heart?"

Casey shrugged. "Not sure. I've never really thought like other people, so maybe that's got something to do with it."

Casey touched the not-Casey's cheek. It burned as though feverish. "Maybe if you flesh out these lines here, you'd look more human."

The not-Casey's eyes flashed anger, nostrils flared, and it recoiled from Casey's touch.

"Here, along the chin, it's like the skin blends into this neckline. See?" She pointed to the mirror for reference. "Maybe your inner heat melts it or something. Your skin's very hot, you know?"

They stood before the mirror. Casey's reflection blinked pale and calmer than Casey felt, but the not-Casey reflected nothing until its colors began to stretch toward the glass like sunlight streaming through a blind. It fanned from the doppelganger toward the glass.

The doppelganger screeched and wheeled on Casey. Its fingernails clawed at Casey's tender skin as it landed atop her in the moist loam. It howled as it slapped and tore at Casey's hair.

Casey rolled into a ball and ducked her head to protect herself from the onslaught. A nasty thump to her head brought a flash of brilliant red and a renewed thud and ache. Scratches burned. Blows pounded. Blood pooled, metallic and salty, in her mouth.

A high-pitched yell ripped through the percussion of attack. "You leave my sister alone!" Little feet kicked the not-Casey from her.

Deirdre held the box in front of the not-Casey as

Sunny chanted in an unfamiliar language. Rachel hunched over her phone, finger thrust into the other ear. A woman's hand reached from the tree line and pulled her from sight. Rachel made a quiet yelp of surprise as she disappeared into the shadow.

When the not-Casey reeled over Malcolm, Casey leaped to shield her brother. "Don't you touch him!" She squeezed her eyes shut in anticipation of the blow from the fiend's attack. It fell heavy as a punishment.

"Don't touch her again, you bitch!"

Casey forced her eyes to slit open. Mom pushed the not-Casey away from Casey and Malcolm. It stumbled back but shied from the trees with a hiss.

Sunny yelled to Deirdre, "It's working! The thing can't leave the clearing."

When it whirled on them, it looked red-faced and formidable, the image of Mom irate.

Malcolm's little whimper emboldened Casey. She reached into the decaying leaves and grabbed a rock over which she'd rolled when attacked. Like David, she let the stone fly. It met the Casey-imposter between the enraged eyes.

Not-Casey faltered.

Deirdre extended the box. Sunny chanted. The doppelganger crashed into the wood and shattered like a dropped looking glass, its pieces silvery shards collected within Sunny's box.

Deirdre struggled with the lid, but it wouldn't close.

An angry wind screamed through. Icy pellets assaulted cheeks and hands.

Casey joined Deirdre as she pushed the lid. It would not budge.

Sunny's voice grew hoarse as she struggled to

intone above the raging winds.

Mom lent her strength to the effort to close the chest. Hinges groaned, but they did not yield until Malcolm threw his weight against it. When it slammed shut, the wind died. Casey's ears rang with its absence. Her heart pounded, and her labored breath gasped. "Is it in there? Is it over?"

Sunny nodded. "We won." She looked and sounded blank with shock.

Deirdre's body shook as she knelt before Malcolm who continued to lean against the chest's lid. "It's gone. Trapped. You did it, kid. You closed the box."

Stretched atop the wooden chest, Malcolm dropped his face onto his arms and sobbed.

Mom thumped to the ground with a groan. "I think I need to go back to the sanitorium for a bit. I think I'm dealing with some things and need a little help." She crossed her arms over her knees, buried her face in them, and cried.

Sunny slid beside Deirdre and touched Malcolm's shoulder. "Little fellow, you have to move now. I have to finish the binding ritual. We don't want that thing getting out again, do we?"

Malcolm ran a fist across his nose and shook his head. He slid off and sidled to Casey.

Mom narrowed her eyes at them but said nothing.

Tromps along the path and Rachel's voice announced the arrival of others. "Over here. Please hurry."

Jaimie and Rachel guided police into the clearing. "Is everything alright?"

CHAPTER THIRTY-NINE:
HOSPITALS AND HOMECOMINGS

When paramedics examined Casey's wounds and suggested a trip to the hospital, Casey collapsed into tears. "Please, no. Please, I can't go to the hospital today." She shook her head with violence and ignored the painful results. "Not now, after everything else. Please just let me go to my room and sleep."

The younger of the two paramedics protested. "Some of these cuts are bad, and we should x-ray to check for concussion." He dabbed the scratches with treated cotton.

Meanwhile, Mom raised her voice. "Excuse me. Did you notice I need some attention? If she doesn't want your help, you should move on to help worthy people who do. Like me." She pointed to her heaving chest.

The older paramedic approached. "Are you hurt, ma'am?"

"I need a ride. I've been dealing with more than any person should have to endure. I'm at my wit's end, and so I think I'll seek a bit of guidance. Please escort me to Dr. Keller." She looped her arms through the arms of the bemused paramedics and guided them toward the campus.

"Mom." Casey's voice quavered worse than her wobbly legs.

Her mother paused but didn't turn to face Casey.

"Thanks."

Her mother glanced over her shoulder. "For what?"

"You stopped her from hitting me again. Thank you."

Mom straightened her spine and turned toward the campus. "Well, you're welcome. Don't forget your mother protected you." She swung her hips as she guided the paramedics along the path.

Her rich voice floated on the cool air. "I saved them all."

Jaimie held Rachel's hand. Casey smiled at them. "Looks like you used your phone for an emergency, huh?"

Rachel's lips struggled between a smile and the trembles of tears. She freed herself from Jaimie and hugged Casey about the middle. She whispered into Casey's thin jacket, "I was so scared." She shivered as she tilted her head up to seek Casey. "Jaimie helped, though."

Jaimie kicked a stone. It tumbled toward a line of pink salt encircling the clearing. "I wish I could have done more to help."

"I have some more questions, ladies." A uniformed police officer tapped a pen to his pad.

Jaimie walked with the officer to tell what she could of the evening's events.

Deirdre helped Sunny gather her things. "Casey, if you're too, um, beat up to drive, I can take Sunny home. If I can borrow your car."

A gentle, cold wind wafted through, carrying a hint of sage and apple blossom. Casey shivered.

Deirdre bent and retrieved Casey's coat. "Hey, here's your missing jacket." She wrinkled her nose. "Might need a spin in the washer, though. Stinks a bit like rotting eggs." Something inside the pocket sounded like a maraca.

Casey pulled from inside honey-colored pill bottles. She locked eyes with Deirdre. "I swear I didn't take these. I'd never invade your space."

"I know."

The pills clanked inside their plastic prisons. "Do you want these?"

Deirdre's head drooped. "I don't think so." She cast a sidelong glance around the clearing. "Not anymore."

Casey concentrated. Deirdre's suicide veil had receded. Casey nodded. "Good. We'll get rid of them once we're back on campus."

"Can I borrow your car?"

"Well, I have to get these guys home, too." Casey placed hands on Rachel and Malcolm.

"Oh yeah, I forgot. Guess I was hoping our security guard would stay the night again."

Malcolm ducked his head, uncharacteristically shy.

Rachel leaned against Casey. "Can we go home now?"

"After the police are finished, I'll get you home."

"I think we're done here, actually." The deep voice of the policeman startled a bat from its home in a nearby tree. It flapped with wild abandon over their heads until it disappeared into the thicker tree line. "We'll walk you to your cars."

With a sibling holding each hand, Casey followed in

their strange parade to the gray cobblestone pathways of the campus, grateful for their utilitarian solidity and familiarity. After a goodbye to the police, the group piled into Casey's car. Deirdre pulled Sunny onto her lap for the trip.

"That's not safe," Rachel pursed her lips.

"We're only going a short distance, and I promise to be safe," Casey said.

Rachel slumped deeper into the back seat. "You're not necessarily the problem."

They made it home without incident, though. After a tearful greeting, Rachel introduced her father and Aunt Hettie to Casey's friends. Malcolm didn't say anything. With a yawn, he climbed the stairs.

"Going to bed, little friend?" Deirdre asked.

Malcolm nodded and continued his ascent.

Everyone called, "Goodnight."

Aunt Hettie studied the base of the stairs he'd climbed. "What upset him so much?"

Nobody met gazes.

Casey cleared her throat. "Mom. She brought them to the campus. At an inopportune time."

Aunt Hettie's face tightened. "Rachel texted they were with your mother at your school."

So glad I got her a phone! "Yeah, but Mom went back to see Dr. Keller."

Aunt Hettie and Dad gaped. "She did?"

Casey nodded.

Dad stroked the stubble along his chin. "What changed her mind? She was pretty adamant about disliking Dr. Keller and the therapies."

Casey shrugged. "I'm not her, so I'm not sure."

Rachel giggled. "As if anyone knows what's really

on Mom's mind."

Casey's friends shuffled, uneasy. "Guys, I have to get Sunny back to her shop and us to our dorms."

Goodbyes and hugs and "nice to meet you's" led to a drive to Sunny's apartment within walking distance of her shop. "I'll walk her to the door. Be right back." Deirdre helped Sunny carry her supplies, including the doppelganger chest.

From the "shotgun" passenger's seat, Jaimie sighed. "She's not what I expected."

"Who?"

Her foot wiggled. "Your roommate."

"What did you expect?"

"Amber said Deirdre was odd, but she's actually really nice."

Casey shrugged. "I like her."

Jaimie allowed her head to drop onto the headrest. "I miss you, girl. I'd hoped you being on campus would allow us more time together. What the heck happened?"

Casey closed her eyes. Vertigo and headache conspired against her will. "Not sure. Maybe we can try harder. Get together more."

Jaimie patted Casey's hand. "I'd like that."

CHAPTER FORTY:
BACK TO THE DEAN

On campus the next morning, Casey received a summons to the Dean's office.

"Again?" Deirdre's eyes widened. "You don't think she'd expel you, do you? Not after we got rid of that doppelganger and all?"

Casey shrugged. "It's not like I can prove anything."

"I'll come with you."

Casey allowed gentle breeze to blow her hair from her face. "You don't have to. I'm becoming a pro at visiting the dean."

"Visiting the dean again? What's up this time?" Newly arrived from class, Tim hurried to carry Casey's bookbag. He kissed the top of Casey's head.

"Everything I told you about on the phone last night, I am guessing."

"Want company?"

"You two can walk me to her building, but really, I've got this. By the way, have you ever listened to The Doors? Jaimie's all into them these days, so I downloaded some of their songs."

She pressed play on her phone as they strolled

along the uneven pathways.

"Of course I've heard of The Doors. Dad likes them." Tim snaked his arm around Casey's shoulders.

Deirdre snorted. "The Doors must be covered in cobwebs by now. Seriously, doesn't Amber listen to anything modern? Like ever?"

They discussed musical merits until they reached the Dean's office. Casey gave them half-hearted hugs. "Don't be late for your classes." She flipped up the collar of her jacket against the playful wind.

As Casey walked away, Deirdre sounded incredulous as she talked to Tim. "Does she really think we're leaving until we find out how this meeting goes?"

The secretary pushed aside a pile of papers when Casey entered the office. "You're back again? I assume Dr. Rosen's expecting you."

Casey nodded.

She tapped the computer monitor. "Oh, here you are on the schedule." She offered an inscrutable stare.

Casey's skin burned under the unflinching consideration.

"You know where the coffee station is. Help yourself." The secretary returned to her labors, and Casey busied herself with the homey task of caffeine prep to will her heart to calm its pace.

"Ms. Adams." A pastel floral blouse brightened Dr. Rosen's no-nonsense pinstriped suit. "Thank you for stopping by. Please join me."

The secretary's covert scrutiny followed Casey's progress into the office. Casey concentrated on keeping her cup level since she couldn't find a lid as her feet sunk into the thick Persian carpet in the

Dean's office.

The blooming pear tree outside of the office window shed white petals. Clouds darkened the sky that minutes before sparkled clear, and the first drops of another spring shower splashed against the bank of glass panes like regretful tears. The progress of one meandered, joined with other small droplets, and picked up speed to disperse at the frame.

Don't overreact. It's not a portent. It's a spring rain.

"I've asked you here to hear of your latest exploits, Ms. Adams."

Exploits? Casey swirled the creamer in a clockwise spiral by rotating her cup. "Um, what do you mean?"

"When last we talked, you and your bunkmate, Ms. Lowry, asked me to suspend the evidence caught on camera and believe you innocent of vandalism and breaking and entering. Campus police tell me they were called to Flagstaff Hill yesterday, and predictably, your name came up. So I ask again, please let me know what new experience you've had on my campus."

The stuffed bookshelves swayed in Casey's vision. *No, I'm rocking.* She forced herself to calm. "Well, I had to trap that doppelganger thing."

"Oh, and did you succeed?"

Casey nodded.

"And nobody was hurt?"

Casey shook her head.

The dean rested her chin on her steepled fingers. "Well, Ms. Adams, I must say your presence on the campus has livened things up. So should I expect some new adventure for the next equinox?"

Casey's head snapped up. "Oh, I hope not!"

Dr. Rosen chuckled. "I must admit, I somehow

suspect this will not be our last meeting of this sort."

Casey's head spun as she joined her friends. They'd taken shelter beneath a gingerbread-laden gazebo off the path, but the rain had since devolved into a fine mist. Jaimie beamed at her and threw her arms about Casey's neck when she entered. She kept a hand on Casey's bicep and tried to disguise her pleasure behind a stern expression. "So, you don't answer your phone anymore?"

"What?" Casey snatched her phone from her pants pocket. Sure enough, it registered a missed call and two messages from Jaimie. "I'm sorry. I must have turned the ringer down."

Jaimie shook her head, unable to maintain a grumpy expression. "I suppose you've had a bunch on your mind lately." She pointed to Deirdre and Tim. "They've been filling me in. So, we're all anxious to know, what did old Dr. Rosen have to say?"

Old? She can't be more than fifty. "She thinks I'll be back in her office in September with another unusual experience."

Tim, Deirdre, and Jaimie exchanged alarmed looks while Casey slid to the wooden bench that ringed the gazebo.

Tim sat beside her and offered his shoulder as support and comfort. He laced his fingers through hers and gave a gentle squeeze. "I don't think we should worry about that. I mean, it's a pretty spring day. The rain's stopped. You're okay. We all are."

Casey allowed his hope to wrap around her even as she harbored misgivings. The sun glistened in a tempestuous sky, and to the east, a pale rainbow struggled from between clouds above what she called

Ceremony Hill. Out of her periphery, something moved, a flash of incongruous autumn in the landscape of emerging pastels. Although it was gone when Casey turned toward it, she knew what it was.

She recognized it by the familiar nausea building in her stomach, in the bile burning her esophagus. By the incongruity of emerging spring overpowered by the scent of autumn leaves incinerated by a blazing bonfire.

The equinox witch.

She disguised her shudder by standing. "Yeah, we're okay. Let's get to our classes before we fail, though."

Tim gave her shoulder a squeeze and kissed her cheek. Jaimie swirled like a ballerina as she splashed in a puddle, a beatific smile transforming her into a Pre-Raphaelite dream, and Deirdre tromped along with them, hands thrust deep into her camo jacket, silent as a shadow.

Casey glanced at the hill where a flash of amber warned the equinox would come again.

SNEAK PREVIEW
OF BOOK THREE

WINTER OF WONDERS

Winter wound its grip around Ol' Nor'Eastern's campus early, closing a frozen chokehold on the little Pennsylvanian town before autumn had relinquished its last vibrant leaves. Tree branches groaned under layers of frozen precipitation. Rock salt crunched on all of the cobblestone pathways and asphalt roads. Ice even glazed the campus pond where a struggle for life and death took place the autumn before.

Beneath what Casey Adams and her friends called Ceremony Hill, students either struggled through finals or prepared for winter break. Casey finished her last final for the semester, but instead of feeling the relief of work-well-done and the pleasant anticipation of the approaching holidays, she worried.

Statistically, more people died over the holidays, and Casey harbored the secret ability of conveying the dead to their next plane of existence.

Someone who reminded Casey of the student who went homicidal last autumn seemed to be stalking her.

But worst of all, her mother would be preparing the holiday meal.

ABOUT THE AUTHOR

Kerry E.B. Black, mom of five young humans, three middle aged cats, and one old dog, lives along a fog-enshrouded river outside the land where George A. Romero's Dead dawned. She dances with words to create intriguing stories, many of which explore the universality of fear. *Awakening at Equinox*, Book One in *Season of Growing* series was published in 2021. Tree Shadow Press has compiled three volumes of this award-winning author's short stories in the books *Herd of Nightmares*, *Carousel of Nightmares*, and *Fairy Herds and Mythscapes*. Be sure to stop by her website for updates on new publications and author events.

www.KerryEBBlack.com

www.ingramcontent.com/pod-product-compliance
Lightning Source LLC
Chambersburg PA
CBHW070748180626
46818CB00007B/3036